FiSH N✦TES and
STAR S✦NGS

CANCELLED

CANCELLED

FISH NOTES and STAR SONGS

DIANNE HOFMEYR

ST. ALOYSIUS COLLEGE S.J.
SENIOR LIBRARY
MILSON'S POINT

60775

BOOKS UNLIMITED 7/05 $14.40 17800

SIMON AND SCHUSTER

To my friend, Clare,
for inspiring so many
readers and writers.

SIMON AND SCHUSTER

First published in Great Britain by Simon & Schuster UK Ltd, 2005
A Viacom company

Copyright © Dianne Hofmeyr, 2005
Cover design by www.blacksheep-uk.com © 2005
This book is copyright under the Berne Convention.
No reproduction without permission.
All rights reserved.

The right of Dianne Hofmeyr to be identified as the author of this
work has been asserted by her in accordance with sections 77 and 78
of the Copyright, Designs and Patents Act, 1988.

1 3 5 7 9 10 8 6 4 2

Simon & Schuster UK Ltd
Africa House
64-78 Kingsway
London WC2B 6AH

A CIP catalogue record for this book is available from the British Library.

ISBN 0 689 87292 5

This book is a work of fiction. Names, characters, places and incidents are either
a product of the author's imagination or are used fictitiously. Any resemblance to
actual people living or dead, events or locales is entirely coincidental.

Printed and bound in Great Britain by
Bookmarque Ltd, Croydon, Surrey

www.simonsays.co.uk

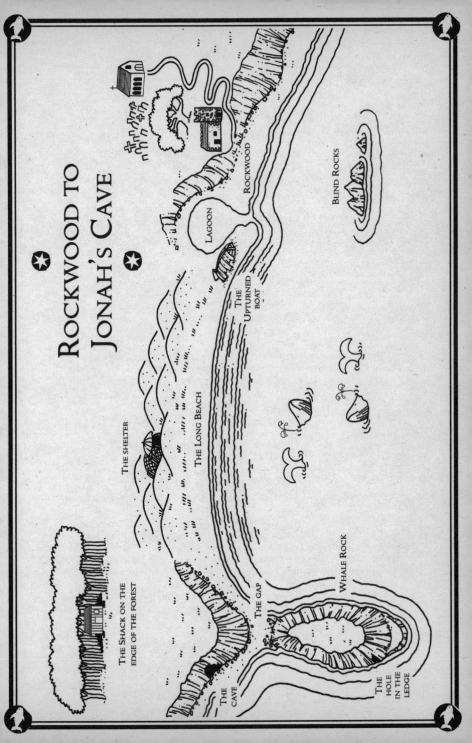

1

Fish Notes

Her delicate skeleton was lifted from the stand on which it had hung for longer than anyone could remember. The leg and arm bones made hollow, musical sounds as they knocked against each other gently. Like bamboo wind chimes in a breeze. For a moment she seemed to be dancing. Her legs moving, her arms lifting and her body swaying to some strange music only she could hear.

She was dancing again after being still for so long.

At least, that's how I imagined it had happened, even though the photograph showed nothing of this.

The heading in the newspaper was in dark print: SARA BAARTMAN HOME AFTER 200 YEARS. Below the heading were the facts. And below them the photograph – the one of her lying in the box she'd come home in.

ST. ALOYSIUS COLLEGE LIBRARY

1

She arrived with very little. Just the box. And two glass jars. That was all.

When I studied the small details in the photograph, I saw that a great deal of careful measuring and marking had been done to make sure she arrived safely. The precise outline of her skeleton and the exact shape of the two jars had been carved into a piece of sponge that lined the box.

Her leg and arm bones no longer danced. They lay still now, neatly held in place in the grooves made for them. And her skull and hip bones settled quietly back into their hollows in the sponge cushion. The two glass jars were taped securely and lay in separate spaces alongside. One jar was filled with her brain, the other with her insides. All shrivelled and grey and floating.

The old label that had been attached to the stand on which she'd hung had been removed. Now, in the photograph, it rested across the rib bones of her chest. I could see the dark, murky ink strokes of the old-fashioned writing. The card read simply:

Sara Baartman - Griqua

I took out my magnifying glass to have a closer look and to see if anything else was written on the label.

Something I might have missed. But no. It was just that. Just the old yellowed label with a small spray of faded ink where the nib had caught in the curl of the 'G'.

That's how Sara Baartman arrived home. With nothing more than that. Just a box, a few bones, some jars and a label to remind us this had once been a person from Africa.

My father's an anthropologist. People interest him. He once spent a year in the desert studying the people who live there. How they built their houses. How they lived. What they ate.

What people eat doesn't interest me. When I saw the photograph of Sara Baartman lying in her box, I didn't think about what she ate. I thought of who she was. I thought of her body. And I thought of her spirit. Without a spirit where was the person?

I looked at the photograph with the bones fitting so perfectly into their sponge cushions. And I looked at the grey things floating in the glass jars tucked alongside. Where exactly in all of this was the real Sara Baartman?

Where was her spirit? In her dusty, brittle bones? Or in her brain in a bottle? Or had her spirit stayed behind in the long, dark galleries of the Musée de l'Homme in Paris where she'd hung with the other bone collections? In the dark corridors with their drawers of skulls and rounded hip bones and delicate finger bones, collecting fingerprints and dust?

Perhaps her spirit had never left Africa in the first place.

The answer to this – and much much more – I found in the cave. In the cave things happened – mysterious, marvellous things – which will disappear from the earth, if no one tells of them. And, once gone, they will be lost for ever.

So I've written it all down in a book, from the very beginning. And across the cover I've written: *Fish Notes*.

But a label isn't enough. It can't tell us all. So the pages of my book are thick and bumpy and curled with everything that had to be written.

On the cover of the book I've painted a fish. What sort, I'm not sure. It's just any fish. Not as ugly as a puffer. But not as pretty as a butterfly fish. It's greenish-pinkish-silver, with yellow dots down its side and fins that stretch out like arms, with a spiny back fin and a small, fanned tail and a dark eye, watching me.

It's just Fish. Like me. That's my name.

But Fish is not my *real* name. It's a name I took.

My father says there are names for different times in our lives. That it doesn't matter what your name is, as long as deep down inside you know who you are and where you come from.

Sometimes I whisper my other name. My real, true name.

I wonder if Sara Baartman ever whispered her true African name. The name she was called in her secret language of clicks that only her own people understood. A name no one knew or even bothered with, when they took her so very far away from home.

For a time none of us knew each other's real names. Why we got them and how we changed them is part of this story. But it's not the *whole* story. There is much, much more.

We knew that day – when the four of us left the paintings and turned our back on the cave – that things had happened there. Things no one will ever be able to explain. In the cave we left behind not just the paintings, but something even more wonderful and mysterious.

On that day, we stood high on the dunes and we

watched the waves crashing in solid lines of foam along the long curve of beach. Then we turned and faced south towards Whale Point. We gave our last look towards the dark shadow of the cave's entrance and the white water licking the rocks below.

We saluted the cave. And all that was hidden inside it.

We stood for a long time, each with our own thoughts and the memory of what had happened there. While we watched, the setting sun caught the cliff-face of the Gap between Whale Point and the beach, and sent back a pink shimmering glow.

I knew then that the mysteries of the cave were still alive.

2

The Arrow

From a distance I saw the thin shape of the arrow against the silvery sand dune. Long and narrow with its tip buried in the sand.

I crept in closer. Glanced over my shoulder. Sea mist brushed my face like a soft rag. Moonlight skimmed the dunes. But no one was hiding in the wavering grasses. And the only sound was the sea sighing softly as the tide went out.

The arrow shaft was damp with sea dew. At the tail end drops of moisture were caught in the feather barbs. They reflected like jewels in the pale, lemony light. The four wings were made of spotted guinea-fowl feathers. Wedged into grooves in the reed, they sat at a stiff angle to the shaft. Four evenly-spaced blades. Not left ragged but cut precisely.

It was an arrow made by hands in no hurry.

A shiver ran through me, reaching right to the tips of my fingers. Who had made it? Were they watching now? Were they out there, somewhere in the strange lemon light between the shadows wavering in the grass?

It was getting late. Already the moon was floating free against an oyster-shell sky. I held the arrow close, turned quickly and ran back along the beach, past the locked-up holiday houses with their blind window-eyes staring out at the moonlight and their tight-shut unspeaking doors.

The air was filled with mist and sea smells. The breath of a million sea creatures. Somewhere out in the bay, the whales were calling. I could hear them. *Ffishhh . . . Ffishhh . . . Ffishhh . . .* The sound came swirling into my ears as I ran.

Out of the corner of my eye I checked the boat still lying at the edge of the lagoon. Stranded, upturned and silvery on the sand. Like some sort of beached sea creature that would never have life pumped back into it. Slowly breathing its last breath in the moonlight.

Across the lagoon below the cliff was the house. The wooden house that stood on stilts. Rockwood. With its garden of pebbles and driftwood and seashells. Built long ago with wood and stone and bits and pieces washed up from the sea by the old Sea Captain, so that it grew in all directions.

Light shone from the windows.

I ran along the wooden walkway, threw open the door and banged it tight shut behind me to keep out the cold sea breeze and the whispering grasses. The ships – painted on pieces of cardboard held up with tacks – bobbed up and down in full sail, jibbing along the walls in the draught.

My father glanced up from his work and smiled. 'You stayed out late!'

The pansy shells leaning up on the shelf and the row of green sea urchins marching from big to small all seemed to smile as well.

'I've found an ancient arrow!'

He rubbed his fingers over the shaft. Then shook his head.

'You mean it's not treasure?'

'Treasure, perhaps. But not old.'

'Not from an ancient tribe?'

'No. The cuts are too new. The feathers too fresh.'

'How do you know for sure?'

'No arrowhead. Look – just sharpened reed.'

'So?'

'Ancient arrowheads were made of stone. Sometimes bone. Sometimes iron. First, a strong reed had to be found. Then scraped and checked for straightness.

ST. ALOYSIUS COLLEGE LIBRARY

Perhaps warmed over the fire to help it straighten. One end of the reed split. Then strong wing feathers chosen.'

'Like these?'

He nodded. 'Yes. Perhaps guinea-fowl. But in ancient arrows, the tip of the quill is cut off. The feather is split carefully down the middle, then cut and trimmed to make four blades. The blades are pushed into the splits in the reed and tied with a leather thong dipped in sticky berry juice to keep the thong tight.'

'And the arrowhead?'

'A flint polished thin and sharp by rubbing against a wet stone.'

'And the poison?'

'Venom – from poisonous snakes!' He pulled a fierce face. Made snake fangs with his fingers and jabbed at my neck. 'Puff adders!'

I brushed his hand away. 'So if the arrow's not ancient, who made it then?'

He shrugged and opened the doors of the Sea Captain's cabinet of curiosities – with the rusty chicken-wire netting tacked across the frames – and laid the arrow down. 'Must fix these doors or the meerkat will get at the bones.'

'You say that every day!'

He placed the arrow on a shelf alongside all the other things. The rocks with fossils trapped in them, the leopard tortoise shell, the ostrich-eggshell necklace, the row of shark's teeth, the collection of long white bones and the dusty journal with its blue and red marble-edged pages.

He picked up the journal, banged it against the palm of his hand to dust it off, then flipped through some pages and began reading.

Thursday August 9, 1894 – Fine weather. Wind light easterly. 65°F. Spied a vessel coming around under Whale Point. Went up the hill to the signal post. Hoisted signals to bring her in and show her where to drop anchor. She signalled back that she was the schooner, the Alfred. *From Swansea, Wales. Come to pick up a cargo of wood . . .*

Over my father's shoulder I read the scrawled note with another date written in pencil in the margin.

No more wood to fetch now. All chopped down to build houses.

'Why did the captain do that?'

'What?'

'Write notes one on top of the other in the margins of his journal?'

'That's what scientists do. They're always discovering more.'

'The old Sea Captain wasn't a scientist.'

'No. A discoverer.'

I looked back at my father, reading his eyes and the smile that touched the corners of his mouth. Was *he* a discoverer? Would a discoverer know where the spirit of someone went? 'Dad . . .?'

'Yes?'

I took a deep breath. Then shook my head. 'It doesn't matter . . .'

'What? What is it?'

'Nothing . . .' I made up my mind then. 'Tomorrow I'll paint the old Sea Captain's schooner. With double masts and seven yellow sails. A mainsail, a foresail, two topsails and three jibs. Up against a dark sky.'

He nodded towards the canvas bag in my hand. 'What else did you find?'

I tipped the shells onto the table. 'Not much. The tide's not right.'

'List them then, while I make mussel soup for supper.'

12

'Twenty-three shells with holes.'

He scowled. 'Scientific names.'

'Twenty-three bivalves with holes. Seventeen molluscs. Mostly *Conus*. A starfish as well.'

'A starfish?'

'Phylum Echinodermata.'

'That's better!'

'A broken pansy shell – *Echinodiscus bisperforatus*. Five *Spirula*. One *Sepia officinalis* from a large cuttlefish.' I tossed the names into the air. There was something magical about saying such words. I tossed them across the room to my father. It was a secret language between us that made us smile.

The wooden floorboards bounced and creaked under my feet. I pulled back the strands of shell curtain that divided the cabin into sleeping and living. The shells made a soft *shirr . . . shirr . . .* sound, like music. From my bunk I could see up into the stone tower lined with shell patterns and tiny broken pieces of mirror that reflected the stars.

My father began to sing the names. He sang them out like an Italian opera into the steamy room. '*Bisperforatus. Conus. Spirula. Sepia officinalis . . .*' He stirred them into the soup like flavouring. Then he laughed. 'And an arrow found in the dunes.'

13

3

The Dune-riders

The girl stood on the crest of a dune. Her eyes as green as the sea on a clear day after the south-east wind. Her hair red against the sunlight. Wild and as straggly as the bushes covering the back-dunes. Wild, as if it had never seen a brush.

'This is our place! You're trespassing!'

The eyes blazed down. She was all in black. A black T-shirt. Torn black jeans. Heavy black boots. Too thick and heavy for wearing on a beach.

'Don't you speak?'

'What?'

'Are you stupid?'

I shook my head.

'Where d'you come from?'

I pointed back towards Rockwood.

'You mean the house at the bottom of the

cliff-path?' The girl narrowed her eyes. 'I've seen you. You live with that man who's always scrabbling for things on the beach.'

I nodded. 'Yes . . . my father. We pick up things washed in from the sea.' I listened as I spoke. Behind me the tide was changing. I could hear the waves pounding as they fought to come in against the water washing out. It was a strong tide. 'My friend was washed up from the sea once.' The words tumbled out. I hadn't meant to say them aloud.

'Hah! People don't get washed up from the sea.'

'She did!'

'How?'

'There was a storm.'

'And . . .?'

Why'd I started this?

'Liar! You haven't a friend who was washed up. There isn't anyone who was washed up.'

'There was!'

'What's her name then?'

Silence. I bit my lip.

'So?' The girl jerked impatiently at the neck of her T-shirt. 'What's *your* name, then?'

'Fish.'

'Fish! Smish! How can you be Fish? Fish swim in the sea. What sort of fish are you? A jellyfish?'

My voice stuck somewhere in my throat.

'Too dumb to speak now? I think you're a sly fish that goes snooping about, stealing things.'

'No.'

'You stole the arrow.' She whistled loudly through her teeth. Two boys appeared at the top of the dune. One was tall. Bare-chested with his ribs showing and jeans held up on his hips by a piece of rope. Skin the colour of honey. A string of small white beads around his neck. The other boy was small. Dark. With huge brown eyes.

The girl nodded in my direction. 'She stole our arrow.'

'I didn't!'

'Liar!'

'I never *stole* it. The arrow was sticking up out of the sand.'

'You'd better give it back!'

'It's in the Captain's cabinet.'

'It's in the Captain's cabinet . . .' the girl said in a sing-song voice. 'Captain! Smaptain! I don't give a shit about the Captain! Bring it back here, Fish Smish!'

I stood, brooding about what to do next.

'Do you hear me? Rebecca says so!'

I put my hands on my hips. Stared back. 'Rebecca who?'

'There's no other name.'

'Everyone has another name.'

'I don't need another name. I'm just Rebecca.'

'And theirs?' It was no good asking the boys themselves. They hadn't spoken a word.

She nodded in the direction of the older boy. 'He's Boy.' Then she nodded towards the younger one. 'He's Boskind.'

'They can't be just that.'

'Why?'

'Boy and Boskind aren't real names.'

'Who says so?'

'Boy means any boy. And Boskind means someone who lives in the bush like a wild thing. They're not special enough to be names.'

'So?' Rebecca shrugged. 'We're the Dune-riders.'

'Dune-riders? Do you have horses?'

'No!'

'What, then?'

'We ride ostriches.'

'Ostriches?'

She nodded. 'Stole them from my father.'

'Stole? From your father?'

Rebecca clicked her tongue. 'Stop repeating everything! We want the arrow back. Do you hear me? Tomorrow or else!'

'Else what?'

'You'll be sorry! We'll come and find you!'

'My father . . .'

'Hah!' Rebecca laughed a small animal-laugh, more like a growl in the back of her throat. 'I'm not frightened of anyone! There's nothing I'm scared of. You'd better understand that!' She grabbed my arm. Looked at me with her fierce green eyes and a scowling face. 'And you'd better bring it!'

Her fingers were digging into me. The nails torn and dirty. Her skin was dark and sunburnt against mine. I looked back into her stormy eyes with their strange dark flecks. This girl was wild. Like some strange wildcat, hissing and clawing.

'Now go!' She released my arm and gave me a sharp jab with her elbow.

Along the edge of the sea the waves were calling *Fish! Fish! Fish!* as they fought their way against the tide. And the wind from the dunes whispered *Run! Run! Run!* The sand caught at my feet. Keep going. Don't look around.

Across the long beach, past the upturned boat and around the lagoon, was Rockwood.

I charged up the wooden walkway and arrived back, hot and out of breath.

'There you are!' My father held up a bucket. 'Look! Black mussels for supper. Got them off the rocks at low tide.'

'We had mussel soup yesterday!'

I could feel him looking at me. 'What's the matter?'

I shrugged. 'Nothing!'

On the other side of the room was the Captain's cabinet with the arrow lying on the shelf. I picked up two wet, dripping mussel shells and held the coolness of them up against my hot cheeks.

'Can people ride ostriches?'

'Maybe . . .' My father laughed.

4

Vanessa

Vanessa is cross. She says I should forget about the girl on the dunes.

Vanessa's my friend. When I went up the cliff-path to speak to her this evening I told her about Rebecca. She said I should keep away from her. That she sounded strange. That she was a liar. That she couldn't live in the dunes because it's cold on the sand at night with sea mists and no trees to protect you.

Vanessa of all people would know that!

I told her about the ostriches and that they were the Dune-riders.

She said it was all lies, lies, lies. That I wasn't very smart to believe Rebecca. She said no one could ride an ostrich. Ostriches were wild things. They would kick and buck you off. And how would they have got the ostriches tame in the first place? And where did they get them from?

Stole them, I told her.

Stole? From where?

Her father.

What sort of person steals from her father? Vanessa wanted to know. And besides, ostriches are turned into feather boas and feather dusters and dried meat. Not horses! Everyone knew that.

I suppose I didn't. Because I really believed Rebecca when she said they rode ostriches. I wished I could ride an ostrich.

I told Vanessa I had to give the arrow back.

See! I told you so! she said. Rebecca is going to give you nothing but trouble. Keep away from her.

She said it very sharply. Could it be that Vanessa was jealous?

She said an arrow couldn't be important. An arrow was just a piece of old stick with some feathers stuck on it. And that I shouldn't be fussed about what Rebecca said. Anyone could make an arrow.

I started to tell her that arrows were difficult to make. About how the first hunters made their arrows. But Vanessa gets impatient with long stories. She said she was tired of hearing about arrows. And tired of hearing about my new friend too.

I said Rebecca wasn't my friend.

21

ST. ALOYSIUS COLLEGE LIBRARY

The words flew between us until my head wanted to explode. So I walked away and left her under the huge milkwood tree.

Words, words, words.

It's hard to argue with Vanessa. It's always words and more words. They swirl and crash in my head like a storm.

I scratched her name in big letters on the beach as I walked along. Slashed them deep into the wet sand. 'V' and 'A' and 'N'. The letters of her name have sharp, spiky points like daggers. Only the 'S'-es have curves. And an 'S' looks like a snake.

Sometimes I hate Vanessa. She makes me angry. So angry I shout at the waves! She's always so smart with her answers. She *always* knows better. She said I should've left something behind when I took the arrow. Like a peace-offering. She said a peace-offering would've been a good idea in case Rebecca was dangerous.

Dangerous? Yes . . . Rebecca – with her wild hair and green eyes looking straight through you – might be dangerous.

Would a peace-offering help to make friends with Rebecca?

A friend would be nice. It gets lonely here. I wish

Vanessa could be friendlier. I wish she could be here with me at Rockwood now. She could sit across the table and help me with shell patterns for the tower.

Vanessa's not always good at shell patterns. Sometimes she lays them out in a wild way that makes no sense. Crazy patterns.

I've seen her get so angry. I've seen her crush the shells in her fists. Crush them until her hands have bled. Then she's taken a smooth round stone and hammered them. Raised the stone and brought it down on each separate shell. She's crushed them all. Shattered them into pieces until they're nothing more than dust.

And even though I close my eyes and shout, 'Stop! Stop!' her hands won't stop.

Then suddenly it's quiet again and I open my eyes and she's gone. All that's left on the table is a fine, powdery mess and smears of blood everywhere which I have to mop up before my father sees them.

Sometimes Vanessa is the wild one.

It helps to climb the ladder into the stone tower lined with its pieces of shell and stuck-down bits of mirror and small windows that look out over the sea. In the round tower I feel safe. A snail tucked into a snail-house.

When I look out at night the stars come back to me reflected a hundred times over in the mirrors all around. So many stars – my head hums with the sound of their singing. Each star has its own place and its own song.

5

The Visit

The house is silent. Just the sound of the sea, swishing against the rocks, and seagulls crying. I dip the brush into a jar of steely grey-blue paint and float the colour across the bottom of the piece of cardboard. Streak and dab it with black and green. This is a fierce sea I'm painting.

In the rough water I outline a flat, brown ship's hull. The Captain's schooner. Yellow sails pulling stiffly in the wind against a huge dark sky. Seven yellow sails. A mainsail, a foresail, two topsails and three jibs. Up against a dark sky. Now the yellow paint is tinged with grey. But there is no time to stop. I drag the brush across the churning waves and around the hull. The whole painting is washed with spray that reaches high into the sky.

Here in this stormy sea I'm at home. No words

needed. Things that swirl and crash inside my head are washed away. The storm in my head and the storm in the painting come together.

Beneath the hull in thin grey watery paint, I outline two large fish.

Not real fish. More mysterious than real fish.

They float, half transparent between sea-colour and spray-colour. Not quite sure if they should be there or not. My brush eases them up out of the stormy water. With a few quick strokes they could turn into sea again. Dissolve and disappear. Sink below the surface under the murky depths.

But no. They're here now. They stay.

Mistakes can be painted over. Yet in a strange way, you know they're still there. If you narrow your eyes to slits, the shapes float back up through the other colours. Like memories.

So now they're here – these mysterious dark fish, swimming alongside me. The waves crash above me. I float in a sea underworld. Being swirled and pulled, this way and that. Feeling the surge of water against my body.

A sharp sound stopped my paintbrush in mid-air. A drip of grey fell onto the ship's mast.

There it was again. *Chink! Chink! Chink!* The sound of small stones pinging against the door.

I held my breath. It was them. I knew it.

I squashed down on the floor and crawled towards the window sill.

All three of them were there. Just standing in the afternoon sunlight. No expressions on their faces. Like people standing in a queue, waiting for something to happen.

I ducked below the window again. Too late. They'd seen me.

'Hey! Fishgirl!'

I kept myself tucked in below the window ledge.

'Fishgirl! I saw you! Open the door!'

Stones pinged against the door again.

'Are you going to open the door or must we break it down?'

'Stop that!' I jumped up. Pulled the bolt aside and stood in the doorway.

Rebecca strode up the walkway towards me. Her boots thudded against the wood. I put my arm across the door frame to block her. The stormy green eyes were up close now. Her face so close, I caught the smell of sardines on her breath.

'Where's the arrow?'

We stared at each other. Then Rebecca gave a sudden sharp thrust with her elbow into my ribs and pushed me aside. She stood with her hands on her hips, looking around the room. 'Jeez! What sort of place is this?' She walked across to the table and flicked open the Captain's old journal.

'Don't touch anything!'

Rebecca snapped her fingers at the youngest boy. 'Keep watch outside, Boskind!'

He scuttled out through the door again. The older boy – the one called Boy – was silently peering into the Captain's cabinet.

Rebecca strode across the room. She ran her hands over the wire netting on the doors. 'What's all this stuff?'

'Collections.'

'Where does it all come from?'

'It belonged to the old man who lived here long ago. It's treasure. From shipwrecks. Fossils from the cliffs. Skeletons of animals and things. The Sea Captain was a collector. The stones are my father's. From the desert. The green is tourmaline. The shiny one's mica. The pink one is rose quartz.'

'He's a grave-robber!' Boy spoke suddenly.

I shot a look at him. He had loosened the catch that held the cupboard doors closed. He was holding a long white bone in one hand and the ostrich-shell necklace in the other.

'I said, don't touch anything!'

Rebecca turned her back on the cupboard. She trailed around the room, sliding her hands over surfaces. She peered up into the narrow stone tower. 'Jeez, what's this? What are the pieces of mirror for?'

'To see.'

'What?'

'The sea and the stars.'

'You can see them if you look out the door. Why d'you need mirrors stuck in a tower to see them?'

'To see differently. In another way. Like magic.'

'Bloody mad! That's what you are!' She picked up the wet painting from the table. 'And this? What's this?' As she held up the painting, two streaks of black paint ran across the sky.

'Leave that alone!'

'The fish are too big. They're bigger than the boat!'

I looked at the silvery gloom of the ocean and the dark horizon. The brave, strong boat and the silvery gleam of the huge, sad fish in the stormy sea. I glanced back at Rebecca. How could I explain?

Rebecca flicked her finger at the cardboard. 'Real fish aren't that big! Even whales aren't that big!'

'They're not real fish.'

'What then?'

'Fish-souls.'

'Fish-souls?' She stared at me.

I nodded. 'Souls of people who get lost in storms.'

'Hah! There's no such thing as a soul!'

'Everything has a soul.' Boy said the words very quietly.

She shot a look at him. 'Who told you?'

Boy shrugged. 'My pa.'

'Your pa's dead! Drowned! Washed off the rocks!' Her words made the same *Chink! Chink! Chink!* sound of the stones hitting the front door.

Boy tugged at the ostrich beads around his neck. I wanted to touch his fingers to stop them from breaking the necklace. I wanted to tell Rebecca to shut up. I slid a look at his face but he wouldn't look at me. 'What did he tell you?'

'Stories from long ago.'

'What about?'

'Of people. The First People. How they lived and how they hunted.'

'Hah! The First People!' Rebecca snorted.

He spun on his heel and faced her. 'It's true. They *were* the first people. And it's true. Everything has a spirit. Even the smallest creature. The moon and the stars have their own spirit. Even a digging stick and an

30

arrow can have a spirit. All these things in this cupboard have their own spirit. Each one. The necklace.
The bones. The tortoise shell. That's why they don't
belong here. It's wrong to trap their spirits.'

I stared at him. Who was this boy? And why did he
suddenly have so much to say?

'Hah! That's stupid! You're talking as weird as
Fishgirl! A necklace and an empty shell can't have a
spirit. This stuff's all dead! Dead as can be. Soon it'll
be dust.' Rebecca snapped her fingers as if she could
turn it all to dust in a flash. 'Dust to dust. That's what
the Bible says.'

'Maybe he thinks—'

Rebecca turned sharply to me. 'No one asked you.
He thinks too much. Won't do him no good.' She
started riffling through the things on the shelf.

'Please . . . don't!' I squeezed between her and the
cabinet.

'You heard what he said. It's wrong to keep all this
stuff.'

She pushed her face right up close. I saw myself
reflected in the green, green eyes. Small and elongated.
With thin arms and legs. Like a strange squid with four
tentacles instead of eight. Tentacles waving about
hopelessly.

31

'Get out of my way!'

There was a flash of silver. She had pulled a knife from the pocket of her jeans. The sharp point was under my chin.

Boy grabbed her wrist. 'Rebecca! Stop making trouble! Put the knife away!'

For a moment she glared back at him. Then dropped her hand.

I felt a warm trickle run down my neck. My fingertips came back red and sticky when I touched the place.

'Just a pinprick, baby smaby,' she sneered. 'Don't mess with me. Next time it might be deeper.'

Boy turned to me. His eyes were dark. 'I'm taking the necklace. It doesn't belong here. It belongs in the cave.'

Just then, there were footsteps on the walkway. The younger boy – the one called Boskind – ran into the cabin with eyes huge, like a small surprised bushbuck. My father came in, carrying a bunch of fish tied together with raffia. He dropped it onto the floor. Looked around.

'What? What's going on?'

No one spoke.

'Fish? Are you hurt? Is that blood on your neck?' He put out his hand. I ducked away.

'Paint, maybe.'

'Who are they?'

'They're from the dunes.'

'What're they doing here?'

'They made the arrow.'

Out of the corner of my eye, I tried to see what Rebecca was doing. I saw the light reflect off the blade. My father must've seen it as well. He swung around. In one quick movement he stopped Rebecca's hand in mid-air. She jumped back. A jar of paint crashed to the floor. The strands of the shell curtain clattered against each other. The knife fell from her hand and skittered across the floorboards, flashing as it spun.

'Jeez! Back off! I wasn't doing anything.' She stood with her back against the wall, her hands clenched at her sides, her hair wild and her green eyes flashing, angry, and as bristling as a trapped wildcat. If she'd had a tail, it would have swished as well.

Boy shot a look at her. 'Pick up the knife, Rebecca! Put it away!'

'Crazy! Crazy! All of you!' She spat the words. Then she scooped up the knife and charged out of the cabin.

Boskind ran after her.

Boy put the ostrich necklace back inside the cupboard.

My father glanced at him. 'Are you Piet's son?'

Silence. Just the sound of the paint slowly dripping from the table onto the floorboards. Boy's eyes followed the drips.

'I heard what happened to your father. I'm sorry.'

He shrugged. 'He was washed off the ledge at the end of Whale Rock. He couldn't swim.'

'What's your name, then?'

'Boy.'

'Boy? Who calls you that?'

He shuffled his feet.

'Well, you can't be just *Boy*. Your name's Jonah.'

I shot a look at my father. 'Why?'

'He lives in the cave in Whale Rock. Right in the mouth of the whale. Like Jonah in the Bible.' There was a smile in the corners of my father's lips. He took a seagull feather out of a jar. I watched as he dipped the end of the quill into the dark paint that lay in a puddle on the table and wrote a date in the back of the Captain's journal. Under it he wrote:

> *Today we were paid a visit by Jonah, the boy who lives in the Whale's mouth.*

Yes, perhaps my father was a discoverer after all.

6

The Thoughts of Rebecca

Bloody hell! They're crazy! Both of them! That Fishgirl and her father are both crazy! I'm not going back into that bloody madhouse with all those creepy things. Paintings with fish-souls! And who-knows-what in that cupboard! And that weird tower with the shells and mirrors. *To see things differently,* she said. She's mad. But I have a knife. And I'm not afraid to use it. I showed that Fishgirl I could use it. A little trickle of blood got her scared! I don't care a shit about anybody. I have a knife. And it's sharp. My pa knows that! Yes, Pa! It was more than a little trickle of blood then. It got him truly scared. I scared the shit out of him that night with my knife! He didn't expect it! He'll never come after me again! Never pull out his belt over me again! Never throw me to the ground! Never again!

She says the mirrors make you see the world in

another way. Like magic. Magic, smagic! Who's she fooling? I see things as they are. The world's *real*. It doesn't matter which way you look at it. There's *no* magic in the world! It's a lie. I should know. There's no magic when you live in a shanty town on the edge of the forest. There's no magic when you scrub, clean and cook. And no magic when you have to dig ice-hard ground for potatoes in the winter with your fingers all frozen dead. And no magic when the potatoes are used up and no one's got a job and you're hungry and you pick arum lilies from the cold wet *vlei* and stand next to the road in the rain but no one stops to buy them because who's going to buy arum lilies when they're growing everywhere and anyone can stop and pick their own. And who wants to stop in the rain anyhow? And no magic when you put your drunken father to bed and you wipe up his vomit. And none when he comes after you with his muddy brown eyes and loose mouth and his scrawny chicken-neck and calls in his syrup-soft voice, Come here, girlie! Come here, Meidjie! Meidjie – which means little maid or little girl. But I'm not his little girl! Meidjie is more like servant. Someone you can order about. Someone who has to do everything you say. There's no magic in a name like that. And no magic when you run out into the forest and hide and hear his stumbling footsteps come closer and closer as he calls. And he snaps the branches and curses. And sometimes he finds you even though you keep to the dark shadows. There's no magic in that. None! And none when you come back to the wooden shack. For where else is there to go? You hope someone will see what has happened. Will reach out a hand and comfort you. But nothing. No one reaches out. Not even to hit the man that walks in behind you.

Magic *doesn't* happen in real life. It's a lie! That's why I used the knife. I showed him that time. He'll have that scar for ever. I'm not scared of him any more! I'm not scared of anyone! His scar will prove it!

7

The Thoughts of the Boy
from the Cave

The girl's father has named me. I'm to be called Jonah. Because I live inside the cave in Whale Rock. Like Jonah in the whale's mouth in the Bible.

I've never been inside a whale's mouth. I'm not sure what it's like.

The inside of the cave in Whale Rock is smooth. Long, long ago, waves washed into this cave. My pa told me. But ever since I can remember the sea hasn't come in here. Not even at full moon when the tide is very high. Or on the day the sun makes its longest journey in the middle of summer. Or in the middle of winter when it makes its shortest journey. The sea's never washed inside the cave since I've lived here.

Even on the day the huge wave swept Pa off the ledge, the sea came nowhere near the cave.

But the rock inside the cave is smooth and shiny. As if it has known water. Smooth as the inside of your mouth.

Further back, deep inside, are ridges like those inside a dog's mouth. And it's completely dark. So dark that when you come in from the sunlight, the darkness blinds you. So dark that dogs stand and bark at the darkness. As if the darkness is a person.

The bark echoes deep inside the cave.

And deep, deep inside the cave is a body.

It lies in the deepest, darkest, most secret part, under a shelf of rock. Half in, half out of the dry sand. Sand as dry as dust. It lies facing the east with a small pile of stones at its side.

Pa said he was our brother. But he can't really be both *my* brother *and* my pa's brother. When I asked about this, Pa said he's of our family from long ago. Perhaps more like an uncle.

From how long ago? I wanted to know. I've never had an uncle before. Nor a brother. Or a sister. Not even a mother I can remember.

Too long, Pa said.

More than ten years? I asked.

He shook his head and laughed. Much, much more.

More than a hundred years?

He nodded. Maybe even more than that.

It's comforting to know we have family in our cave.

At night in the darkness I lie in the front part of the cave. I think of this man lying deep, deep inside. The pounding sea echoes inside the cave so loudly it seems it will rush in and wash both of us out. Although I know it won't. It hasn't before. So why should it now? I think of this man and I wonder if he once slept in the very same place I sleep now. In the front part of the cave. There's a smooth hollow here. It seems just right for the shape of a person. As if many people have slept in this same place.

I've lined the hollow with pieces of *buchu* bush. Then I've covered this with cloth so the leaves and stalks won't prick me. The sweet smell of the *buchu* is soothing. It sends me dreams. In my dreams, my brother-uncle comes to me and tells me stories of what it was like to live hundreds of years ago.

Now that Pa has gone – washed off the rock into the white foam sea – my brother-uncle still talks to me in my dreams. So I still have family even though Pa has gone. I look into the face of my brother-uncle who is not my brother, nor my uncle, but someone who lived more than a hundred years ago, and I whisper his name.

Pa gave him a name. A name with its own magic. It needs time to think and dream about.

Heart Fire.

Heart Fire is the Day Star which appears in the sky every morning before the sun. It's the star that travels in front of the sun. So by day we don't see it. But it's there all the same. It's the fire that brings warmth to our hearts.

Heart Fire. I hold his name close to my heart to bring me warmth.

Sometimes I creep deep into the cave. I look at his bones and the way he lies half on his side, with his legs curled up, and I wonder if he was cold when he died. The cave is cold in winter, especially when the south-wester blows rain straight off the sea.

He has a torn, leather skin that covers his hip bones like a *kaross*.

Pa said not to touch it, or it would turn to dust and his spirit would be disturbed.

So I don't touch it.

I bend down very close and look and see the fine folds in the leather skin. This piece must have been rubbed very soft before it covered my brother-uncle.

It's hard to know what animal it came from. I look down at my torn jeans. I think of how comforting it must be to have the skin of an animal so close to your skin. Surely the spirit of the animal must enter your own body. I long for the touch of a skin. An antelope skin, so I can run as swiftly as the wind. An eland skin, so I can be the bull that commands the thunderstorms. A lion skin, so I can be a brave hunter.

But I don't touch the skin.

Above and all around my brother-uncle are the paintings on the rock. Although he lies in the dark he must know they are there. The paintings tell stories from a time long ago. He must dream of them in the darkness.

Pa and I set candles down on a rock ledge. The paintings are high. Pa lifted me onto his shoulders. We stretched our necks to look.

In the yellow candlelight the colours of the paintings are soft. The legs of the people and animals dance across the roof of the cave. Men carry quivers filled with arrows on their backs. There is a man with a white antelope-head. A huge eland bull snorts smoke from its nostrils. Fish and turtles swim out from a crack in the rock.

Up close I see shadows of other paintings, floating

beneath the top ones. It seems people have painted in this cave for a long, long time.

Next to Heart Fire is the pile of stones. They're his sacred stones. They mustn't be moved. Every ancestor who has ever visited his grave has put a stone there. Some have come from far away. I can tell by their shape and colour. They're unlike any you find here.

My fingers itch to pick them up. To feel the weight of them in my hand. To explore their smoothness or their roughness. So that by holding them I can sense the river bed or high mountain or dry plain from which they've come.

But the stones must be kept sacred. So I don't touch them. Even though my fingers itch.

Pa and I added our own stone to the pile. It was smooth like an egg, with a band of purple that ran through the grey stone. It came from the gully in Whale Rock where the sea rolls the stones backwards and forwards until they look like gulls' eggs.

Before I put it on the pile, I held the stone in both hands for a long time so the stone would take on the warmth of my heart. Heart Fire. So my brother-uncle would know it was *me* who put it there.

Around his neck are ostrich-shell beads. Very fine with their edges chipped off to make small, round

ST. ALOYSIUS COLLEGE LIBRARY

discs. They're creamier and darker than my own. My necklace is made from new ostrich shells. Pa made it when we bartered a fish for an ostrich egg from a farmer. Pa took the egg and, with a sharp stone, made a tiny hole at the top. On the opposite side he made another hole. Then he blew hard against the top hole. Suddenly the insides came streaming out of the bottom hole, into a bowl he'd put underneath. We stirred it up with a stick and cooked it over the fire in a pan. It made a mixture that seemed like twenty chicken eggs.

He chipped the shell into beads afterwards. One by one. Into tiny discs, no bigger than half the size of my smallest fingernail, with a hole in each one to thread on to fishing line.

In the girl's house is another necklace. A much older necklace. It doesn't belong there. How did they get it? Her father's a grave-robber. Grave robbers steal the mysteries of the ancestors. They put them in cupboards for people to look at.

They rob the ancestors of their spirit.

8

Vanessa

Vanessa said I was stupid to let them in the house. She said I should've known they'd cause trouble.

I picked her a bunch of flowers today. Pink geraniums, growing wild on the dunes, and papery blue ones that smell like pepper. I put the flowers in an old glass jar.

When I showed her the cut under my chin where Rebecca had held the knife, she said, See! I told you so! This Rebecca girl is dangerous!

Something's puzzling me. After they left Rockwood, the arrow was missing.

It was Rebecca, Vanessa said. Rebecca sneaked off with it. You shouldn't trust her.

I get tired of Vanessa being so clever, so I changed the subject. I told her about my new ship-painting with the stormy sea and the two fish – which was now spoilt because of the streaks of wet paint that had run all over the sky and sails.

For a while Vanessa was quiet. She makes me feel uncomfortable when she's quiet for a long time.

Two fish? Did you say *two*? she eventually asked.

I nodded.

Not one?

I looked hard at her then. She knows my hand paints what's in my head.

Yes, *two* fish-souls! Not one!

There was silence between us. I listened to the sound of the wind sighing through the heavy leaves of the milkwood tree. Some days the sound makes me shiver.

When it had been silent for too long and I was beginning to wish I wasn't there, to break the silence I told her about Jonah's new name.

Jonah? She rolled the sound of his name around in her mouth like a little smooth stone she wanted to taste. Then she smiled and said she'd a feeling Jonah was special.

I felt put out that she called him 'Jonah' so easily. As if she'd known him for a long time. When of course she hadn't. When I told her how Jonah's father was washed off a rock ledge while he was fishing, she blocked her ears. She said didn't I know she didn't like to hear about people drowning?

Of course I understood this. And said I was sorry.

Then she asked what had happened to the other boy. The younger one.

I said I didn't know. He had vanished into thin air.

You haven't told me anything about him. Or what he says.

That's because he never says anything. He's always silent.

Maybe he's not real then.

What do you mean, 'not real'?

Well, he never speaks and he disappears. Maybe he doesn't exist. Maybe he's in your imagination. You know you're good at that.

Good at what? I asked.

Imagining things.

Yes. Remember the time we were doing patterns with the white mussel shells? When you said they were flying butterflies.

But they *were* like butterflies, with two wings still hinged together.

But they weren't *real* butterflies. They were just shells.

I know that!

47

So why did you say they were butterflies?

I was pretending.

You're always pretending!

Sometimes I hate Vanessa.

When I walked away, she muttered under her breath that I was stupid to let someone as dangerous as Rebecca into the cabin. Vanessa always likes to have the last word.

Words, words, words. Always words.

They go around and around in my head.

9

The Thoughts of the Boy
from the Forest

I don't speak not because I *can't* speak, but because I don't want to.

All the words I want to say will not help.

So I don't say them.

If words can't help you what's the use of saying them? I don't need words any more.

All the words I've ever known have flown away. Up, up, up into the trees. Like birds. They've disappeared into the silent leaves.

For all I know they might've flown straight up through the leaves, right out of the forest, into the sky. Or maybe the words wove themselves into nests for birds to sit in.

In any case they're gone now. All the words I've ever known.

Gone!

I don't have to speak ever again!

Not to my pa. Not to anyone.

No more words.

My name was a word, once.

S-E-B-A-S-T-I-A-N.

It's a long word. It sounds like wind teasing the trees. Whispering, whispering.

I hold the whisper in my head. It's easy to remember.

When I look for worms in the soft earth of the dark woods and scratch behind bark for termite eggs, the trees whisper my name back to me. *Ssssebastian . . . Sssebastian.*

It's an easy sound for a tree.

Sssebastian . . . Sssebastian.

Now I can't forget it.

Trees have their own language. It's very easy. If I put my ear against the trunk of a tree, I hear the tree talking to me. I hear it like my own blood. I hear it breathing, too. I feel the warmth of the bark against my ear and I listen.

Some trees are tired. Especially the really big ones. Their sap flows slowly. So tired, they sigh. Others are young and strong. They make so much noise while they're growing. You can hear the leaves growing inside their branches.

Under my feet the earth talks as well. It tells me its secrets.

It tells where a caterpillar is hiding, tied up in its nest of silk.

It tells where the spider has laid her eggs.

And where the ants are going.

Ants are always friendly. You never see ants fighting. They walk up to each other and say, Hello, how are you? Then when they have touched feelers they walk on again.

It would be nice to be an ant.

Ants don't have fathers.

My pa says, What are you doing just standing there, leaning up against that tree? You should be finding wild honey for us. You should be looking for birds' eggs.

I can't tell him the trees are talking to me.

Or that my feet are listening. Listening to things under the leaves. And smelling the sweet earth-smells of ancient trees rotting beneath me.

Or that the ants are telling me where they're carrying their food.

If I told him he would beat me.

So I tell him I'm listening for bees to guide me to the honey.

Always listening! Always bloody listening! Stop bloody listening and find!

I don't like finding.

I don't like taking birds' eggs. I don't like stealing honey from bees.

Worker bees work hard to make honey. They do bee-dances to show where the nectar is. They tell each other by flying in a special way. People think they're just buzzing about. But they're doing bee-dances to show where the nectar is. When they store the nectar, they flap their wings. So fast you can't see their wings. Then nectar turns into honey.

My pa doesn't call me Sebastian. He calls me *Bastiaan!*

He says it like the swear word.

Not like the wind in the trees.

Each sound separate and sharp like a bee sting.

BA! STI! AAN!

Bees don't mean to sting you. They just don't want you to take their honey. The only way for them to tell you is to give you a sting. They don't really want to because, after they've stung you, they die. So it's not very nice for them. But they're trying to protect their honey. So bees don't mean to sting you. They can't help it.

My pa says my name as if it's meant to sting. Each sound separate. Sharp.

Names can easily be broken.

You have to carry them carefully.

He couldn't break me with his stick. But he broke my name.

Each time the stick came down across my legs, it made a sweeping sound.

BA! STI! AAN!

BA! STI! AAN!

BA! STI! AAN!

I don't have to listen.

I can make myself very small and silent.

When I am small, I roll up like a caterpillar that has been touched.

I roll up into a tight little round coil.

I lie on the rotting leaves of the forest and smell the sweet earth smells.

I can be as small as a beetle or a grub creeping under the stones between the roots.

I don't have to hear him.

I don't have to speak.

I am so small he can't see me any more.

I am smaller than the smallest ant.

Tinier than the tiniest bee grub.

I have disappeared.

I don't feel the stick.

I am small.

Small.

Small.

I am inside myself.

I disappear.

10

Barter

The sun was hot on my skin. The wooden steps warm against my legs. In the bay the fishing boats were going out. Quietly. Quietly. Creeping out over the shiny sea with the seagulls weaving patterns above them against the sky. The sea was flat. Like glass.

I curled my fingers to my thumb to make a spyglass. Put the spyglass to my eye. Framed the upturned boat lying next to the lagoon. 'When're we going to take the boat out again?'

Silence.

'Summer's coming.' I glanced over my shoulder at my father. He didn't look up. 'Dad?'

'One of these days.'

'But when . . .?' I put the spyglass to my eye again and searched the beach for any sign of Rebecca or Jonah or the small boy.

Far away the whales were calling . . . *Fisshh . . . Fisssh . . . Fisssh . . .* Soon, they'd be leaving. Deep down under the sea, they'd know summer was coming. They'd sense the light on the water. Feel the earth tilting closer to the sun. Know it was time to leave. Time to go south to where the icecaps had begun melting.

'Why do they have to leave?'

'Who?'

'The whales. Why can't they stay?'

'They don't go away for ever. They'll be back.' I sensed my father's eyes on me. Looking for clues. Trying to read the thoughts in my head.

But I didn't turn around. I couldn't say the words out loud: Mum won't be back, will she? What is it when you don't come back? What is dead? Just lost? Or gone for ever?

I swept my spyglass over the sea again. There was nothing there. Then I moved it over the beach. In the circle of my fingers, a figure appeared. Walking closer and closer until he filled the circle. He was coming towards the cliff-path.

'A visitor,' I announced.

'Who?'

'Jonah.'

56

He stood at the bottom of the boardwalk in silence, with some green-backed mackerel hanging slithery and fresh from strings of raffia in his hand. He was wearing a long-sleeved blue check shirt with a red T-shirt underneath. He looked strangely different. Formal.

My father came to the door and stood behind me. 'Ah, Jonah. Straight from the Whale's Mouth! Mackerel, I see. Are they a gift?'

Jonah shook his head.

I glanced from one to the other as they spoke over my head.

'Are they to buy?'

He shook his head again. The fish dripped watery stuff from their gills onto the wooden walkway. Flecks of fish scales glistened on his hands in the sunshine.

'To barter?'

'Yes.' Jonah nodded. His eyes darted through the doorway past my father towards the Cabinet. 'I want the necklace.'

'What?' My father squinted back at him.

'The ostrich necklace.'

'Why?'

'It belongs to my brother-uncle.'

'Your brother's uncle? Who's he?'

Jonah shook his head. 'I can't say.'

'You can't just demand the necklace!'

'I'll give you the fish.'

My father laughed. 'Do you think a little bunch of fish will earn it?'

'What will, then?

'Courage and knowledge.'

'You robbed a grave for it!'

I shook my head. 'That's not true, Jonah! He didn't!'

He shot a look at me. 'He's got bones in there. Your father's a grave-robber! Grave-robbers steal the spirits of the ancestors.'

I jumped up from the steps. 'No. The bones are from the Captain's collections, from long ago.'

Jonah didn't budge. His high cheekbones and mouth were carved stone.

My father peered at him from under his bushy eyebrows. 'Come inside, Jonah.'

Jonah hesitated a moment, then he put the fish on the steps and stepped through the doorway.

My father picked up the old journal from the table. 'This is how the necklace was given to the Captain. He earned it as a gift.' He flipped through, came to a page and pushed it towards Jonah. 'Here, read this.'

Jonah looked away. I glanced at him. His face was glowing.

'No matter. I'll read it.'

Sunday June 20, 1894 – Wind NW. Fresh breeze, increased to a gale by 10pm. Lightning and thunder. Wind terrifying. House stands firm. At midnight a knock on my door. Rain sweeping in as I open to discover Enoch standing there, drenched. Came to call me to attend his child. Says I have special medicine. I tell him I have none but he insists I come to save her. Went in the pelting rain to his shelter where the child lay. Child very hot. Bitten by a scorpion, they report. Brown or black? Can't say, they reply. In the rain I searched for the special herb bushes. Made a pack of them. Placed them on the girl's leg. The heat finally left her. Enoch looked at me with an eye that said he saw something else. I grew quite frightened and asked him, What? He said he saw the shadow of the scorpion crawling out of the girl as I bent over her. Candlelight, I thought. Just candlelight. Maybe the lightning. Shadow and dark. Late at night. Who can tell?

My father stopped reading and looked up. 'So, Jonah – what do you think?'

Silence. Jonah's eyes were on one of the paintings. It was my boat painting. The one with four masts.

'So . . .?' my father asked again. 'Was it a real scorpion that crept out of her?'

'I wasn't there.'

'Yes, but what do you think?'

'I think the spirit of the scorpion was inside the girl. Her father saw it leave. The Captain's medicine made it leave. Spirits of things have a way of showing themselves when the time is right.'

'How do you know?'

Jonah looked at my father. 'There are things you can't explain. You just have to believe.'

'Do you believe the old man took the scorpion from her?'

'She got better, didn't she?'

My father nodded.

'Then he took it from her.'

'But how?'

Jonah shrugged. 'Perhaps he was a healer. A shaman.'

My father reached for the string of ostrich beads in the cabinet. 'The necklace is yours.'

I stared at him. 'Why?'

He laughed. 'Be patient, Fish. Knowledge isn't given on demand. It's something mysterious that's shown you. Jonah has earned the necklace as a gift.'

11

The House in the Dunes

I elbowed my way through the dune grass. Creeping along on my stomach. Hardly breathing. Just before the top of the dune I stopped and glanced over my shoulder. The air was very still. No rustling in the grass behind me. Just the dull thud of the waves far away.

I'd brought along a piece of mirror, to hold above the tips of grass like a periscope. To see what was happening without being seen. I twisted it this way and that. It reflected nothing but sand dunes and grass. No sign of Rebecca.

A seagull swooped overhead. Its shadow ran over the sand like a small grey meerkat scampering for cover. Then a spark of light flashed across the sand behind it. My heart jumped. It was the reflection off my mirror. Had she seen it?

Suddenly there was a dull thud behind me. My face

jerked forward into the sand as someone grabbed my feet. I struggled to turn and see. It was Rebecca, pinning down my arms and sitting astride me.

'What're you doing, Fishgirl? Why're you wriggling through the sand like a snake?'

I twisted around. She was wearing the same black jeans and there was a bulge in the pocket where her knife was kept. My heart throbbed right in my ears.

'I asked you a question!' She looked at me with angry slit eyes.

'I was just looking.' I tried to bury the piece of mirror in the sand.

'Just looking? Spying, you mean! Is that what the mirror's for?'

I shook my head.

'You're a little snake, aren't you, Fishgirl? Not even brave enough to take the arrow out of your mad Captain's cupboard.'

I twisted as hard as I could, kicked my legs free and lay back on my elbows in the sand, glaring at her.

She had braided her hair with strands of dune grass. At the end of each braid, she had tied a spotted guinea-fowl feather. They danced around her neck and cheeks as she moved. She looked like some strange, exotic bird.

ST. ALOYSIUS COLLEGE LIBRARY

'Cat got your tongue?' She reached into the pocket of her jeans. Her fingers fumbled with something. She pulled out an old dented tin.

It wasn't the knife after all.

She popped the lid off with her thumb. Inside were some loose shredded leaves and some cigarette papers. She squatted down on her haunches, tipped some shreds onto a piece of paper and rolled a cigarette. Then she ran her tongue along the edge of the paper to stick it down. She struck a match, drew hard and narrowed her eyes through the smoke. A sweetish smell drifted through the air.

'You're such a baby! Why don't you go back to your mummy, baby smaby?'

My face was suddenly boiling. Burning hot. 'Because . . .'

'Yes?' Rebecca tilted her head back and blew smoke into the air without looking away.

I shot a look at her. 'My mother's dead. Drowned.'

'Bloody hell! Not another drowning story! First your friend. Now your mother. Well I'm not going to feel sorry for you! You know nothing about troubles, Fishgirl. Nothing! You've never had to look after a dirty stinking father.' She took another deep draw on the cigarette. 'Why're you spying?'

'I wasn't.'

'What then?'

'I wanted to see where you lived.'

'What'll you give if I show you?'

I shrugged.

She grabbed my wrist and put her face up close to mine. 'Listen here, Fishgirl, d'you think you can come here and have a look for nothing?'

Silence. I bit my lip.

Rebecca clicked her tongue. 'OK! Don't go blubbing on me now. I'll show you. But then you owe me. A favour for a favour.'

I kicked at the sand. 'What sort of favour?'

'I'll decide later.' Then she laughed. A harsh laugh in the back of her throat. 'Maybe a forfeit's better.' She jumped up as if she'd suddenly decided. The guinea-fowl feathers ruffled out around her face.

I shook the sand out of my hair and dusted my arms and legs. Then I glanced over my shoulder. If I was quick I could still run away.

She grabbed me by the arm. 'Come! Follow me!' Then she laughed again. 'I dare you!'

I walked behind her through the dunes into the *fynbos*. It was quiet. We were in a dip beyond the dunes. Whale Rock was completely hidden. No sound of the sea here. Just the sharp, tangy smell of the bush and the first summer cicadas singing, a few guinea-fowl cackling nearby and, from somewhere deep in the undergrowth, the hollow insistent call of a *boubou* shrike.

'There!' Rebecca pointed. 'Do you see it?'

There was nothing. Just a tangle of bush scratching my arms and legs.

She pulled aside a branch of twisted wild camphor. Behind it, an old faded-pink Coke umbrella with rusty spokes pointing in all directions was pushed into the sand. Attached to the umbrella was a shelter made of scraps of green and black sheets of plastic tied over a frame of saplings. Here and there, bits of wire gripped the plastic like giant staples. An old beach towel with a faded starfish was draped over a bush and nearby was a grey, broken deckchair.

'Welcome to my holiday house!' She ducked under the umbrella and disappeared through an opening between the plastic. I crouched down and peered in.

'Come on!' She pulled my arm.

There was a pile of ash near the opening and a smell of wood smoke. Inside, it was like a nest lined with scraps. Some pieces of blanket and bits of cloth and old clothes lay scattered around. The light from the plastic reflected a green gloom. A picture of a rock band was tacked to a branch. Next to it was a small photograph of a woman. The kind taken in a slot-machine booth. It was blurred and difficult to make out the face.

'See! Everything we need! A pot for cooking. A plastic bucket for water. Blankets to sleep on. An axe. It's surprising what people leave outside their houses at night. When we're tired of it, we'll leave it all behind and move on. We're free.'

'And then?'

She shrugged. 'What's it matter to you?'

'How do you get money?'

'Hah!' She picked up the axe thumped it into the dirt floor. 'Questions! Questions! Always questions!'

'What about your family?'

'See what I mean?' She glared at me. In the green shadowy light her face was a mask. Then she hacked the axe into a sapling. The shelter shook. 'What about them? I hate my pa. I'm never going back.'

'Don't any of you go to school?

'Hah! Jonah's never gone to school! He can't read or write. And Boskind's too young.'

'And you?'

'Me?' She looked at me through angry slit eyes. 'D'you think I'm stupid, Fishgirl? Hey?'

I shrugged.

'Listen, I spent seven years at school. I know what I know. I'm finished with school. I can read and write.' She rolled another cigarette. Its tip glowed as she puffed at it. 'Have a draw?'

I shook my head.

'Go on, baby smaby! I dare you!'

'Stop calling me that!'

'What?'

'Baby smaby!'

'Don't tell *me* what to do! *No one* tells me what to do. You hear me?' She cleared her throat and spat through the opening of the shelter. Then she laughed and her mouth twisted. 'I'm finished with taking orders. Finished with lots of things. But I'm not going to spill my guts out telling you everything I've seen, learned and done in my life. I won't tell you about living in a squatter's shack at the edge of the forest with a pa who's always drunk. No, you don't want to hear about this! Just know I've finished with lots of things, baby smaby!'

'I said, don't call me that!'

Silence. Her eyes glinted ice in the shadowy green light. 'And I said, don't get smart with me, Fishgirl.' She spat a piece of tobacco off the tip of her tongue.

'You don't listen, do you? I don't like orders. Remember, I have a knife. And you're far from home.'

I sneaked a look over my shoulder towards the opening.

'There's no one here to protect you!'

I wet my lips. There was a bitter taste in the back of my throat. 'Where are they?'

'Boskind's taken water to the ostriches.'

'And Jonah?'

'At the cave.'

Silence.

'Scared now, aren't you? Scared there's no one to save you? Wish you'd never come?'

'I'm not scared.'

'Well, you would be if you had any sense! See this place?' She looked up at the framework of saplings with plastic clinging to them. 'Built it all myself. Chopped the wood with this axe.' She hacked into the sapling again. 'Cut the branches with this knife.' She flicked open her hand. A blade snapped out from the handle.

'I've cut throats with this knife. Do you believe me?'

I listened for the tread of footsteps in the undergrowth. For the sound of the sea. For anything. But there was nothing. Just silence. Not even the screech of the cicadas or the cackling guinea-fowl now. Even the *boubou* shrike had gone silent.

Just the thump of my heart and Vanessa's voice. *I told you . . . I told you.*

'You don't believe me? Well, I have.'

I squinted back up at Rebecca. Ice in her bones. Vanessa was right. This girl was dangerous. 'I do.' My voice was a whisper in the back of my throat.

'That's better, then!' Rebecca gave her strange animal laugh with her mouth all twisted. 'Because if you don't believe me, I'll have to show you. Have you seen a chicken with its head chopped off? It flaps around even though the head is lying in the sand and blood is oozing everywhere. It's the same with an ostrich. They kick and run wild without their heads. I've cut the throat of an ostrich. Chopped the head clean off.'

I watched Rebecca's face. Thought of those huge, feathered wings beating against the air. Beating and beating. And the blood spurting. I felt my own blood throbbing and a sticky hotness collecting on my skin.

'Do you believe me?'

'Yes . . . yes I do.' My voice was hoarse.

She smiled suddenly. 'You know, I like you, Fishgirl. You're a baby but you're different to most baby smabies. Go home now, Fishgirl. And remember, no telling your pa about this place. I don't want him snooping around and checking up on us. And sending me back to school. Remember, you owe me a favour.'

'What sort of favour?'

She shrugged. 'Don't know. A favour, or a forfeit. I'll see when the time comes. Go now!'

I wriggled out through the opening into the fresh air and stood up. I sensed her eyes on my back. There was a blurred movement and a soft thud. The knife handle quivered as its blade struck sharply into the sand at my feet.

Rebecca laughed her throaty animal laugh. 'How about that? I could've sliced off your foot.' She snapped her thumb against her finger. 'Just like that! What would you have done then?'

Don't stop. Just walk. I heard Vanessa's voice.

'Hey, Fishgirl! I'm talking to you. What *then*?'

On the sand I saw my foot lying off to one side like a chicken-head. And me hopping about on one leg. Bleeding. Bleeding like a chicken without a head. Blood everywhere.

'What would happen, Fishgirl?'

I looked at her then. Wet my lips. Forced the sounds out. 'I'd bleed to death.'

'That's right. All alone here in the sand dunes. You'd bleed to death. You're not stupid either. Now go!'

My heart was screeching louder than any cicada. Don't run. Just walk. And don't turn around. Don't look back. The dry leaves crackled under my feet. Ahead was a dune. Behind that was the sea.

12

The Cave

It was a long walk across the beach to Whale Rock.

Huge waves thudding in sent explosions of spray high into the sky and whipped up lines of creamy foam along the sand. Stranded bluebottles, jellyfish and broken bits of red crab lay caught in the foam necklaces like blue sapphires and glistening moonstones and twists of orange coral.

Two oyster-catchers ran ahead on the wet sand, with red beaks and button eyes gleaming in the sunlight, pecking at bits and pieces.

At the far end of the beach, I ducked under the fence that closed off the nature reserve and took the fishermen's path over the rocks. Here, on the other side of the Gap, the giant Atlantic rollers were crashing in against the warm Indian Ocean. The wind whipped tears into my eyes. My hair streamed out on either side of my head.

This was a wild, desolate place with swirling gulls and screeching cormorants, and heavy sea-spray and rocks tumbled and hollowed by the stormy sea. Strange to think of Jonah living here, all alone.

Across the cliffs was the dark slash of the cave opening. A line of thick foam clung to the rocks below. The small beach at the base of the cliff was swept clean and free of footprints. No sign of him here. Nor anyone else. Just a cormorant perched on a rock drying its wings. Holding them stretched out like the spokes of an ancient, broken, black umbrella.

I climbed over the rocks down to the beach. The sand was ice under my feet, the light white and dazzling. Dancing on the sea. Bouncing off the rocks. But against the cliff, the cave was a black slit. Darker and deeper than I remembered when I'd come here once with my father. The darkness sent shivers through my bones.

I stood at the opening with the huge curve of rock arching high over me and the sound of the waves hissing back at me. Bracken and icy drops of water dripping from above. The sides of the cliff rising up it as if to crush anything that dared enter. What was there in the darkness?

As if in answer, a mass of black shapes suddenly swooped out and swirled around my head. The breeze of their wings brushed my face and the noise of them echoed far back into the darkness. Not bats, but swallows. Along the outer edge of the cave I saw their mud nests.

I stepped forward, out of the sunshine into shivery darkness and felt the goosebumps rise on my arms and legs. Gradually, my eyes got used to the gloom. If Jonah lived here, there was no sign of him. Just a few fish bones and some rusting cans which could have been left by picnickers. At the back the cave narrowed into inky blackness.

A torch. Why hadn't I brought a torch?

Then something moved. My fists clenched in a ball. Light flashed against luminous eyes. My heart froze. A round, furry thing charged out past my feet.

'Bloody hell! Stupid dassie! Stupid bloody animal!'

Suddenly a voice boomed from the darkness. 'Fish?'

I jumped. 'Jonah . . .?' His name echoed back strange and hollow. 'Damn it! Jonah! You terrified me. Where are you?'

'I'm over here. Come!'

'Where . . .? It's so dark.'

'Your eyes will get used to it.'

I crept forward. The sea smell had disappeared. There was a sharp, musky smell like animal droppings. 'Are there rats?' My voice was a hollow whisper.

'No. Only dassies.' Jonah lit a match. 'See, nothing. Just dassie droppings.'

In the flare of the match I saw strange earth-marks drawn on his face. 'Jonah . . .?' Then the flame went out. 'Your face . . . what're those marks?'

'Nothing!'

Silence. Only the muffled echo of sea against the cave walls, the musty smell and the slow drip of water.

'Just marks. I fell.'

'You didn't fall. Give me the matches. Let me see them.'

'No.' Then silence again.

'Jonah?'

'Can you keep a secret?'

I nodded. Then realised he couldn't see me in the dark. 'Yes.'

'I want to show you something.' He took my hand.

I gripped it tightly as I stepped forward into a wall of blackness. So dark I wanted to duck my head to avoid bumping into it.

'Get on your stomach.'

I opened my eyes wider, trying to force them to see.

'Come on!' He clicked his tongue. 'It's clean.

There're no droppings here.' He pulled me down.
'Follow me.'

'Why?' Again I was whispering.

'You have to.'

I felt him get down alongside me. The next moment
he let go of my hand and was gone.

'Jonah . . .?'

'Come on!' His voice was muffled. 'Lie down. You
have to squeeze through. There's an opening. It's easy.'

I lay flat on my stomach. The smell of the earth
trapped against my face. I traced along the base of the
rock with my fingers and felt the way it dipped under.
Behind me was darkness. Ahead of me was darkness.

'Put your head to one side. Wriggle your shoulders
and elbows. Come on, Fish. You have to.'

'Why? Why do I have to?'

'I want you to come. I want to show you something.'

I held my breath and squeezed under the smooth
rock, my fingers scrabbling for a grip, the rock cold
against my body.

'Let go.' His voice was somewhere below me. 'Slide
down here.'

I plunged into the void.

Jonah was waiting at the bottom in a circle of light.
There was a candle on a ledge. From the drip of wax I

saw it had been lit many times before. There was a thick, heavy silence. Like the breath of a huge beast. I tried to fill my lungs. If the flame was burning there had to be oxygen.

'Where are we?'

'Inside Whale Rock. My pa and I discovered it by accident.' He smiled. 'Come.' He disappeared down a passageway, into darkness.

'Waitttt – *Jonahhh???*' I listened to the echo.

The cave was deeper than I'd imagined. This is how bats flew. By echoes. My skin began to prickle. Heart-beats throbbed against my chest. Concentrate on breathing. Slowly in. Breathe in calm. Slowly out. Breathe out terror. One foot in front of the other. You can do it.

There was a dim light ahead. Then the darkness grew lighter. We were in another, wider cave. Jonah was standing in the middle of it holding the candle. He pointed to a place high up on a side wall. 'Look!'

There were marks there. Perhaps the outline of something.

He lit another candle on a ledge and handed it to me. 'Get up on my shoulders.' He crouched down, held out a hand to grip mine. I swung my leg over his shoulders. Then he stood up and caught his balance. I clutched the candle in one hand and held onto his forehead with the other.

Up closer, I saw they weren't just marks. It was a painting in dull reddish brown of an old sailing ship with four masts. Each mast had sails and a flag. Outlined in rusty red, the ship had waves around it and a fierce wind blowing the sails.

'See . . .' Jonah tilted his head up to look at me. 'It's like your ship painting. But painted with earth colours instead of paint, and with brushes made of reeds and feathers.'

'It must've been done by sailors who were ship-wrecked here long ago.'

'No.'

'Why not?'

'The four flags fly differently. The flag on the right flies in the opposite direction to the other three.'

'So?'

'That can't happen. Flags fly the same way when the wind blows.'

'What does that mean?'

'My pa said this shows the person who painted the ship wasn't a sailor. Sailors would know about flags.'

'Who painted it, then?'

'Someone who watched the sailors arrive. Someone

who lived here long before, who'd never seen a sailing ship before they arrived.'

'But who?' I tried to pull Jonah's forehead back so that I could see his face.

'My ancestors. They were here long before the first sailors came from Europe.'

'How do you know?'

'Because these are all theirs.' He took both my hands, stretched out his arms for balance and turned, slowly.

In the candlelight our shadows bounced out in front of us against the cave walls. But they weren't the only shapes. Other shadows were already there. Paintings everywhere. Of people and animals. Delicately painted in rusty ochre and pale cream. Their long, thin legs leaping. Their necks stretched out. Moving around the cave walls as if they were dancing. Heavy eland bulls with delicate legs and strange half-men, half-animal creatures.

'Some aren't just men. They've animal heads and animal feet.'

'They're shamans. Healers. It's a spiritual dance. In their dreams they call up the power of an animal. They become that animal. Their spirit-animal.'

Silence. Just our shadows swaying over the dancing people. Dancing with them.

'Jonah?' I looked down at him but couldn't see his face. 'Has this got something to do with the marks on your face?'

'Perhaps.'

'What?'

'Can you see the lines of light between the figures?'

I screwed up my eyes and looked hard. Yes. I could see them. Thin bright lines painted in yellow earth that twined like a cord between the people and animals, connecting them to one another. As if the people were leading the animals or perhaps the animals were leading the people. It was hard to say. 'What are they?'

'It's spirit power. The men are leaving their human bodies and becoming spirit-animals. The spirit lines lead them through this world into the sky where our creator lives. The paintings are a joining with the spiritual world.'

'A joining?'

'The paintings have joined the men with their spirit-animals and with the creator.'

'And the bulls?'

Jonah shook his head. 'They're eland. Sacred antelope.'

My eyes followed the faint yellow lines winding between the men and the antelope. It was like following the lines of a maze puzzle. I studied them through half-closed eyes. Suddenly the puzzle fell into place. 'Look, Jonah! The men are holding onto the lines like a rope, but some are also walking along them. As if the lines are pathways.'

I could feel Jonah nod. 'Yes, perhaps that's how it is.'

'What?'

'A rope or a pathway – whichever way – the threads of light still connect them to the creator.'

I needed to see Jonah's face. I loosened my hands from his grip. Put them on either side of his head and tilted his face upside down towards me. There were dark smudges under his eyes and a white streak across his nose. His cheeks were dabbed with spots of white and dark. Even from upside down, I could see I was looking at the face of a wild animal.

'A leopard! That's what you are! Your spirit-animal's a leopard!'

'No.'

'But you've spots on your face.'

'Yes, but what colour are the marks under my eyes?'

'Dark.'

'Exactly.'

'What, then?'

Jonah laughed. 'A leopard has *white* marks under his eyes to help him hunt at night.' He crouched down and eased me from his shoulders. He put the candle down on a ledge.

I stared at his face. He was a spotted animal with dark stripes under his eyes. Dark stripes to keep the sunshine from reflecting into his eyes. So he wasn't a leopard. But an animal that hunted by day. What then?

'A cheetah . . .?'

'Yes!' His eyes flashed yellow. 'Yes, a cheetah. Now sit and I'll play you my cheetah music.'

He took down a wooden bow from the ledge. The kind you use to shoot an arrow. Except this wasn't one to hunt with. A taut gut was tied from tip to tip. He plucked the gut twice with his thumb. A strange sound echoed through the cave. He smiled at me. Then with the yellow candlelight catching his eyes, he rested the bow under his chin against his throat and plucked again.

I watched his fingers flutter up and down the string. He was making it hum.

Against the cave walls the sound echoed and grew until it filled the space. I closed my eyes and listened. I'd never seen a cheetah in real life. But now, inside my head, I could feel it. This was a cheetah walking. Walking quietly. Pads softly falling on the ground.

Stalking. Now faster and faster. The cheetah was running. Slicing through the grass. Chasing.

When I opened my eyes again, sweat was gleaming on Jonah's skin. His fingers fluttered and jumped and sprang over the bow. He seemed to have forgotten I was there. Suddenly he gave a final pluck. The sound quivered in the cave for long afterwards.

Then, silence. Nothing more. Just the hot, heavy animal-breath silence of the cave and the candlelight flickering over the paintings and over Jonah's gleaming skin.

Finally he looked up at me.

'You're like these people in the paintings – aren't you, Jonah? A shaman.'

He shrugged.

'What then?'

'I dream of becoming a healer. But you can't just take it. It's something given you. You're born with the soul of a shaman. I long for my spirit-animal. But it has to find me.'

'I think it has.'

'For your spirit-animal to find you, you have to prove yourself.'

Does everyone have a spirit-animal?'

He nodded. 'But they don't always find it.'

'Mine must be a fish.'

Suddenly he laughed. 'No. Your spirit-animal is something else.'

'What?'

From the ledge in the rock he took out two hollow oyster shells. Some dark stuff lay inside one and pale creamy stuff in the other. He spat into one and rubbed his fingers inside the shell. Then he came up close. I closed my eyes. Felt the warmth of his hands against my face. He smudged his thumb in an arc across each eyebrow. He paused for a moment, and then he drew his thumb from the centre of my forehead down the length of my nose.

When I opened my eyes I sensed dark shadows above my eyelids. Then I squinted down. There was a dark earth line running along the ridge of my nose and white clay marks on either side of it. They seemed to make my nose longer. I looked back at Jonah. Tried to read the reflection of my face in his eyes.

'What am I? I whispered.

'A gemsbok.'

'A desert antelope?'

He nodded.

'Don't be stupid, Jonah! I'm not from the desert. I'm from the sea.'

ST. ALOYSIUS COLLEGE LIBRARY

He shook his head. His eyes were luminous in the candlelight. The colour of clear gold honey. Cheetah's eyes. I tilted my head back to see him properly. As I did, I sensed the weight of two heavy black horns at the back of my head. Instinctively I put my hand up to feel them. But there was nothing there.

13

Vanessa

It was hard to convince Vanessa.

A gemsbok?

Yes.

That's crazy! See what I mean, Fish?

What?

You're always imagining things. Letting your imagination run away with you. First you hear star songs. And now you say you're an antelope.

But I *felt* them. I felt the weight of the horns.

Fish! You come from the sea.

I know that, of course. It's hard to argue with Vanessa.

This is where you belong. Vanessa said it in that accusing way. As if I was being disloyal to her. Then she looked hard at me. Do you know where gemsbok live? They're from the desert. They don't live anywhere near the sea. They live in the red sands of the Kalahari Desert. Far from here. Where there's nothing but sand. No people. Nothing. Whenever you see a picture of a gemsbok, they're standing all alone on a red sand dune, with their black and white faces turned and their black horns pointing to the sky. There're never any people with them. They're always alone. Just a huge curve of red sand behind them. Not a tree or anything.

I looked at Vanessa trying to think of something. Then I remembered. They don't live alone, I said.

Who says so?

My father. They live in the desert with the Khoisan people.

No one can live in the desert. There's no water.

They have sip-holes where they sip up water from under the ground through a grass reed and then squirt the water into an ostrich-egg shell. They put stoppers in the eggs and bury them to keep them cool and store the water like that until they need it.

That's disgusting.

Vanessa was annoyed. For once I knew more than her.

You should look in a mirror, she said. You don't have anything growing out of your head. Not even the slightest hump. In any case, gemsbok are huge, strong animals. You're not huge. And not even the slightest bit strong.

But that's how I felt.

See what I mean. You're always imagining things. Vanessa started to hum then.

Why're you humming?

I'm not humming.

You are. I can hear you.

Go home now, Fish.

I looked at her then. What? She's never told me to go home before.

Go home. I'm busy.

Busy with what?

The humming went on.

I said, busy with what?

You have to go now, Fish. You have to leave.

But I don't want to.

You have to. It's time to leave.

14

The Thoughts of the Boy Who Does Not Speak

I follow the girl. I creep along behind her. She doesn't see me. She walks along the beach but I follow at the edge of the dunes. I run like a shadow. She doesn't see me following her.

I follow her everywhere.

I followed her to the house in the dunes. I watched from behind the bushes. I saw Rebecca throw the knife but I knew Rebecca wouldn't hurt her. I followed her to Jonah's cave. I waited for her in the shadow. Afterwards, she ran up the cliff-path past her house.

Between the blue morning glory creepers she runs, through a mist-jewelled spider web that stretches across the path. I hear the sound of the threads snapping. A sound like buttons popping off a shirt.

There are puff-adders in the creepers along the path. She doesn't see them. But I know they're there. Puff-adders are lazy. They lie in the warmth of the sun. Thick and fat. And do not move. They look like big branches lying there on the ground.

If you stand on one, they bite your ankle. Not because they hate you. But because you've given them a fright. They don't like you to stand on them. Then you get big and fat and swollen just like them. Except your heart stops and you die.

I am not afraid of puff-adders. You just have to be sure not to stand on them.

The girl doesn't see them. She walks on.

I tell the puff-adders not to lie on the path in her way. I tell them not to harm her.

I'm not even afraid of the rinkhals or the scorpions that live here.

The rinkhals is a spitting cobra. It comes up hissing with its head up high. So high it stands almost on the tip of its tail. Its tongue goes flick . . . flick . . . flick.

I stare into the yellow eyes of the rinkhals. And it knows not to poison me.

I say, Scorpion, scorpion put down your sting. And its curved tail drops.

And so both the girl and I went up the cliff-path without a worry.

I heard the butterfly wings as they swooped around our heads.

They were happy in the sunshine. Happy with the smell of the morning glory flowers.

The girl came to the stone arch with the huge bell and the wooden gate.

I followed.

On the gate are big letters. An 'S' for Sebastian. And 'E's and 'T's as well.

But the letters on the gate don't say Sebastian. They say the name of the church, SAINT PETER'S. I know this not because I can read, but because Rebecca has told me the name of the church.

The girl walked along the pathway to the graveyard. She passed all the graves except the last one at the end. The new one. Here she stopped. She bent and scooped up old flowers from a glass bottle. She filled the bottle with fresh water from a tap and put in new flowers.

There are words carved into a stone cross on the grave. I can read some of the letters but not all. So I don't know these words.

She sat at the grave for a while. Then she walked on and I followed. We came to a green cave. Not a true cave but a huge tree with branches coming down very low and scraping the ground. Inside it was dark as the forest on a rainy day. In the middle, the trunk of the huge tree spread its branches everywhere. Like a skirt.

I listened at the edge of this dark green place. I felt the sea shuddering under the earth even though the sea was far below. And I heard the leaves of the tree whisper my name.

I stood like a shadow at the edge of this place and the girl didn't see me.

15

Greenfire

That evening all three of them were waiting at the door of Rockwood.

'Come,' Rebecca said with a sideways twist of her head. The braids and guinea-fowl feathers had gone now.

'Where to?'

'Jonah's caught some fish. We're going to cook it.'

'Where?'

'On the beach.'

'Fires aren't allowed on the beach.'

'Who says so?'

'There's a sign.'

'I don't care about signs. In any case, Jonah and Boskind can't read. Are you coming?'

I glanced over my shoulder at my father. He smiled and nodded. 'Yes, go. I think you'll see greenfire tonight.'

We went down the path to the sheltered corner just below Rockwood. The tide was in. Spray was jumping where the rocks jutted out into the sea and mist was hanging in the air. My father was right. There was a strong sea smell. The smell that told you there'd be greenfire in the waves when it got dark.

Boskind ran off to collect driftwood. Jonah put three fish down on a flat rock.

Rebecca took out her knife. 'I'll gut them.'

'They're my fish! I'll do it!' Jonah squared his shoulders.

She shot a look at him. 'Yes, but it's *my* knife!'

He turned his back on her and picked up a dry branch caught between the rocks. Snapped it hard. He went on snapping without speaking until the pieces were small. He piled them up, lit them with a match and blew to get the fire going. There was a smell of wood-smoke as the flames started curling and crackling upwards. Then he walked away without saying anything. His straight back showing how cross he was.

Rebecca laughed, then ripped off her jersey, flung it down and went down towards the sea. She ran her thumb over the blade of her knife, spat on it, then swiped it backwards and forwards through the wet sand. Then she came back and swiped the edges against the rock. Back and forth like a sword-fighter preparing for battle. The sand between the rock and blade made a gritty sound. Set my teeth on edge.

She tested it against her thumb again. Looked up suddenly and laughed. 'Sharp enough to cut an ostrich's neck.' She clasped a fish by its tail and scraped against the scales. Little flakes of silver jumped in all directions and settled on her arms and in her hair like sequins.

'Want some jewels, Fishgirl?' She thrust her hand down the fish's gullet. A frill of red gills came out in her fist. She held them under my face. Her hands red with blood. The blood dripping through her fingers. She draped the fringe around her neck like a necklace and laughed. Little trickles of blood soaked into her T-shirt. Then she wiped her hands against her jeans and went on scaling the other fish.

Jonah returned with more wood. He eyed Rebecca and her red gill-necklace but said nothing as he fiddled with the fire.

Rebecca took a few onions from her pocket. 'Compliments of the Spar Supermarket! I would've taken potatoes, too, but the security guard was eyeing me!' She pushed them around the edge of the fire and used a stick to drag some embers on top of them. Then she sat cross-legged on the sand and looked around.

'Where's Boskind?'

He was sitting on a rock holding a shell to his ear like someone listening to a voice on the telephone.

'Hey, Boetie! Come over here next to the fire! Come and sing for us!'

I glanced across at her. She always called him Boskind. Now she was calling him *Boetie*. Brother? I looked from one to the other. Yes . . . perhaps. I hadn't seen it before. Vanessa might've noticed something like that. But I hadn't seen they were brother and sister.

Rebecca pulled the boy towards her. 'Come sit with me.' She bent forward to look into his face. 'Hey, Boetie? Why don't you sing any more for your old sis? Remember how you used to sing to me? Remember when we sat outside the house on the edge of the forest and the huge fires we used to build? So big that the whole sky crackled with sparks. Remember that time when Pa was gone for a while? When Ma was still there and we sang? Remember? You used to sing like a little bird. But now you've lost your voice. Come sing for your old sis again. A nice sweet song to make us all happy. Come on now, sing a little.'

Jonah shot a look at her. 'Leave him, Rebecca! He'll sing when he wants to. When the time is right.'

But she wasn't paying any attention to Jonah. She was whispering things in the small boy's ear. He sat silent and still until she tickled him, then he laughed and cuddled against her. When she looked up I could see her face was soft in the firelight. Different.

Jonah beat the embers down and laid the fish on them. A smell of sea came from them as they started to cook.

The darkness had come down on us. Rebecca sat like a queen in the firelight, her red jewel necklace still clinging to her neck, fish-scale sequins sparkling in her hair and her arm around the small boy, singing softly under her breath.

There was a faint sound of humming. No more than a murmur. It was coming from the small boy. A sound that was hardly a sound. More like a breath beating in the back of his throat as he lay with his head in Rebecca's lap, looking up at the stars.

In the dark I lay back on the sand and listened. Perhaps he hadn't lost his voice after all. Perhaps it was just his soul that had forgotten how to speak.

Suddenly, the small boy pointed upwards.

I sat up. 'Quick! A falling star! Make a wish, all of you!'

We watched the light streak across the sky and fade

over the sea. Then I turned back to the firelight and looked around at their faces. 'Do you think it's a sign?'

'Hah!' Rebecca shot a look at me. 'A sign for what?'

Across the fire Jonah nodded. 'The star is a sign that a heart is falling. Stars know.'

I searched his face. 'Know what, Jonah?'

'Stars know the time at which we die.'

'How?'

'When a star falls, a heart dies.'

Rebecca looked at Jonah with her night-piercing eyes. 'Jeez, Jonah! That's rubbish!'

'It's not!' Jonah argued. 'A star fell that evening.'

'When?' Rebecca demanded.

'The evening the wave took my father. When a heart falls, a star does too. The star's noise dying away takes our heart with it.'

I watch Jonah's face as he says this. My own heart seems to be slipping away. I nod. He sees me nod and smiles. I look into his eyes and I know what he thinks. That there are things out there. Things that have to be said, so they can be placed in the air. Even if people don't believe them, they still have to be told.

'Death? A falling star means death?' Rebecca tossed

her head. Just like a queen would toss it. The starlight was trapped in the fiery red glints of her hair. 'That's a lie. I've never heard a star! Stars don't make a sound!'

'They do!' Jonah said firmly. 'Just because you say so, doesn't mean it *is* so!'

Rebecca went on singing as if she hadn't heard him.

It was then that I saw the waves sparking green luminous light. 'Look, magic!' I whispered. 'Greenfire! All along the edge of the waves!'

Rebecca stopped singing and gave me a look. 'Fishgirl, you think everything is magic! But it's not. It's just stuff in the water that shines in the dark!'

I hugged my arms close to my chest. 'Yes . . . I know. Phosphorescence. It's the phosphorus in microscopic sea-creatures that have been washed into the bay. But it's still magic for it to have collected here tonight especially for us.'

Rebecca laughed. A deep laugh from the back of her throat. 'You're mad, Fishgirl! Mad! Mad! Mad! Such words! Such crazy words!'

Jonah jabbed a stick into the fish. The juices ran clear. He lifted them carefully from the fire, one at a time, holding another stick underneath, and laid them down on a rock. Then he rolled the onions from the embers. The outsides were burnt black and papery.

We ate the sticky fish straight off the rock. Pulled bits off and sucked the hot flesh right off the bone. Then we peeled off the black papery parts of the onions and tossed the pale insides from hand to hand until they were cool.

'Don't burn yourself,' Rebecca said as she blew on a piece and offered it to Boskind.

Yes, this was a different Rebecca. Someone I hadn't seen before. She was a wildcat that had suddenly pulled back her claws.

I licked and sucked my fingers until there was no more sweet juice left on them. I studied Rebecca's wild ginger hair and green cat-eyes in the firelight. Then I looked across at Jonah, 'What d'you think Rebecca is? What's her spirit-animal? Is she a leopard? A wildcat? Maybe a lynx?'

He wiped his mouth with the back of his hand and peered at her. 'None of them.'

Rebecca tossed her head. 'I'm a *lion*! That's what I am.'

I looked across at her. Yes, she was a lion. Green-eyed. Fierce. Ragged and harsh. With rich fur. A tawny, gold, mahogany-maned lion. And then I looked at the arm draped across the boy's shoulder. No, she wasn't. She wasn't a lion.

'No, you're not. Lions are always fierce. You're not always fierce.'

'Hah! That's what you think, Fishgirl!' She pushed the small boy aside and jumped up. 'Let's see who's the bravest!'

'I didn't say you weren't brave. I said you weren't always fierce! It's different.'

'Well now, let's see who's the bravest. Let's swim out to Blind Rocks.'

Jonah clicked his tongue. 'Rebecca, sit down. It's too dark to go swimming.'

'No, let's swim. Come on, Fishgirl. Swim with me. I'll race you to Blind Rocks and back.'

I looked across at the water and the green waves coming in out of the dark, like ripples of light. I thought of swimming and the water pressing down on me. Felt my chest tighten and tried to breathe. Don't panic. It's not going to happen. You're not going to have to swim. You're not under water. I gulped at the air. Perspiration prickled around my neck and in the palms of my hands. I sensed Jonah looking at me. Saw Rebecca waiting for my answer.

Dark shadows loom around me. There's a shape in front of me. Just beyond my reach. My lungs are bursting. The water surges. Takes the shape away. I see it going. See it disappearing. I fight to reach it but it's gone. I should've reached it. Should've swum with that shape.

'Fish?' I hear Jonah's voice. I blink. Bring myself back to the moment.

Rebecca is standing in front of me, waiting for an answer.

I shake my head. 'There're sharks at night. You shouldn't swim at night.'

'Hah! Rules again! You're always making rules! Shit-scared, you mean! Well, *I'm* not!' Rebecca ripped off her jeans. She ran down to the water's edge in her T-shirt and panties and called back over her shoulder. 'Come on, Jonah! Come on, Fishgirl! Watch this!'

The sound of her voice caught in the wash of sea breaking on the sand. She splashed in. The small boy ran after her and stood at the edge of the waves. The water turned silver-green on either side of her as she dived. She kicked up a trail of greenfire. In the darkness you couldn't see her arms or her head any longer. Just the luminous sparks of green splashes as she swam.

I put my hand to my mouth and shouted. 'Rebecca! Come back!'

But she didn't.

Boskind was stamping greenfire footprints in the wet sand. They stayed like magic, for a moment, and then slowly faded away. I wanted to be small again and stamp along behind him. Stamp away my fear. Feel the greenfire magic between my toes.

We stared at the trail of silver-green in the sea. Then suddenly there was silence and the sea went dark at the place we were looking at.

Rebecca had disappeared.

I shot a look at Jonah. 'She's gone!'

Then I peered hard at the dark water again. She was playing tricks. How long could Rebecca hold her breath? I began counting. Slowly . . . so it was like seconds passing . . . fifty-five, fifty-six, fifty-seven, fifty-eight, fifty-nine . . . One minute. She had been down one minute.

'Jonah, what if something's happened?'

He took hold of my hand. 'Nothing's happened.'

'A shark could've got her. Pulled her under. By now she should've reached Blind Rocks. She should've turned back. But there's nothing. You must go after her, Jonah.'

He shook his head. 'I can't swim. Maybe you should.'

'Me? No, you don't understand. I haven't swum since . . . not since . . .'

'What?'

Suddenly there was a sound behind us and cold things dripping down my neck. I spun around. 'Rebecca—?'

She gave her hoarse, throaty laugh and shook drips out of her hair just like a dog that's been in water. 'Scared the shit out of you, didn't I? You thought I'd disappeared. I swam back underwater, then came out quietly onto the rocks over there and ran back along the beach. I saw you standing here, staring out over the sea. Fooled you both.' Then she tousled Boskind's head. 'But not my Boetie. He came to find me. He was waiting at the rocks.'

She linked her arm into Jonah's. 'But I scared the shit out of the two of you!'

Jonah pulled away. 'That's not funny, Rebecca!'

'Come on, Jonah! Don't be so cross tonight! Come! Race you back to the fire. Let's build the biggest fire ever. Let's dance. And then tomorrow . . .' But she didn't go on. She just smiled up at him.

I looked from face to face. There was some secret between them I didn't understand. I kicked the sand. 'Tomorrow? Tomorrow what?'

'Tomorrow we're going on a secret journey.' Rebecca grinned. 'I'll fetch you, Fishgirl!' Then she charged back to the fire with the small boy at her heels and began to click her fingers and stamp her feet and sway. She danced in circles. Stamping and clicking around the fire, her voice rising up high and clear above the sound of the sea.

16

The Journey

The next morning Rebecca leaned against the door-frame with the sunlight making orange fire around her hair. 'I've come to fetch you, Fishgirl.'

'What for? The forfeit?'

She shook her head. 'Want to go somewhere you've never been before?'

'Where?'

'Yes or no?'

Silence.

'You can ride up front on the ostrich.'

The green eyes gave nothing away. She was back to being a wildcat.

'Scared to come?'

I shook my head.

She narrowed her eyes. 'What, then?'

'I'm not scared.'

'Not scared of what?' She gave her throaty animal laugh. 'Me? Or the ostrich?'

'Not scared of either.'

'Prove it.'

'I don't have to.'

'Why didn't you swim with me last night?'

I bit hard against my lip. I wasn't going to blurt it out. 'I don't have to tell you!'

'You know what, Fishgirl? I think you're shit-scared! I think you're shit-scared of most things. But you don't want to show it!' She burst out laughing. 'But still . . . I like you, Fishgirl.' She turned on her heel and gave me a look. 'Are you coming?'

Half of me wanted to stay where I was. But half of me needed to follow her and discover where she was going. So I went down the cliff path behind her.

The ostrich was tied to a post at the edge of the beach. It eyed us with sharp twists of its neck and made hissing noises at the back of its throat.

'Shut up, Og!' Rebecca pulled off her jersey and threw it over the ostrich's head. 'That'll keep her calm. Here!' She crouched down and cupped her hands together to make a stirrup. 'Step up. Pull yourself on. Hold tight once you're up. If you fall off, she'll trample you!'

I shot a look at the huge clawed toes raking the sand

with deep cuts.

'Come on! Hurry! Grab hold of her wings.'

It was like clutching two gigantic feather dusters except they were warm.

'Dig in with your knees. And hold tight! We're going on a journey you've never been on before. To a place you've never been to before.'

Rebecca untied the rope and swung herself up behind. She stretched past me to grip the long neck and pull away the jersey covering the ostrich's eyes. The bird shot forward and I started to slip. Rebecca grabbed the back of my jeans. Then she stretched her arms around on either side of me and clung to the ostrich's neck with both hands.

We went at a wild gallop down the beach. The lagoon skimming past the corner of my eye. The sand and sea rushing towards us. The houses with their blinking windows blurring. The whole world sweeping past. I closed my eyes. Held on blindly. Felt Rebecca's breath at my ear.

'Keep holding. Og knows where to go. We've done this before.'

I felt her arms on either side of me. Felt her laughing against my back. A wild, delicious laugh. Suddenly, I was laughing too.

ST. ALOYSIUS COLLEGE LIBRARY

The salt air tore tears from my eyes. We were racing the full length of the beach. Going faster than I could believe. Tearing along. Everything a blur. Sea and sand. Blue and white. Our crazy ostrich shadow-shape racing alongside us on the sand. The waves crashing around us. The wind pulling at me. Turning my hair into whips around my face. My heart racing.

I wanted it to go on for ever. Then, suddenly, we were at the end of the beach, next to the huge bulge of Whale Rock. Without warning, Og pulled up abruptly. We fell off into a heap on the wet sand. Still laughing.

Rebecca rolled onto her stomach. 'Enjoyed that didn't you Fishgirl?' She gathered a ball of sand, packed it tight with both hands and threw hard. It splattered against my arm with a sharp sting. When I brushed away the sand there was a red mark.

I jumped up and shot a look at her. 'Why?'

She squinted up at me into the sun. 'Why what?'

'Why did you have to throw it so hard? And why do you always do it?'

'Do what?'

'Always have to show how tough you are. Like last night – swimming off in the dark, just to prove something. I'm tired of you. I'm tired of you always having to prove something. Always, *always* having to be the bravest and strongest!'

She lay flat on her back with her hair in the wet sand and laughed. 'Because I *am* the bravest and strongest!' Then she suddenly sat up again with a serious face. 'But you know what? I'm not tired of you, Fishgirl. I like you. Here, want some licorice?' She shoved a hand into her pocket and brought out a strand of twisted black licorice.

I stared back at her. She could change herself as many times as a snake changed its skin. A snake! That's what she was. Her spirit animal was a snake. She had all the anger of a hissing snake. She wore her anger like armour – armour linked as tight as the scales of a snake's skin. Then suddenly, it was as if she'd forget to be angry. She'd burst from her skin and became another creature. I studied her face. She was smiling now.

'Go on! Have a piece.'

'Where'd you get it?'

She laughed. 'It was a forfeit. From a shop.'

'You mean you stole it – like the onions?'

She shrugged and laughed.

The licorice was warm and sticky, with bits of sand stuck to it. It tasted salty like the sea.

She bent over and looped a length of rope around Og's leg and around the post of a rusted notice that read:

WHALE ROCK NATURE RESERVE

NO ENTRY HERE

Then she stood up. Pushed back a tangle of wet, sandy hair and smiled at me. 'Come on! We're going to Jonah's cave.'

I followed her. We ducked below the broken fence and went along the fishermen's path. Then we turned up over the rocks towards the Gap. Boskind was already waiting at the other side. He stood below on the small patch of sand in front of the misty entrance to the cave. When he saw us coming, he ran ahead and the darkness swallowed him. We climbed down into the shadow and the darkness swallowed us as well. Icy cold and clammy after the bright sunshine.

When we came to the low shelf I'd crawled under before, I heard Jonah's voice from the other side of the rock. 'Slide through.'

I crawled forward on my elbows, the musty earth smell against my face, trying to remember exactly where the gap was. I led the way so Rebecca would know I wasn't scared. Then, suddenly, a light flickered on the other side. I rolled into the void and landed at Jonah's feet. He stood there holding the candle and smiling.

I heard Rebecca grunt as she dropped down beside me. Boskind followed like a shadow. Then Jonah led the way through the tunnel until finally we were in the huge cave. The cave of paintings. I glanced at Rebecca and Boskind. But they weren't acting as if anything was unusual. Rebecca was sitting on the sand rolling a cigarette. She lit it from the candle flame.

'So, Jonah?' She drew deeply. Its tip glowed in the shadows. Then she blew out and passed it on to Jonah. 'I told Fishgirl you were going to show her something different.'

He took a deep draw on the cigarette then passed it back.

Rebecca looked at me. 'Want some, Fishgirl?'

I shook my head. 'Show me what?'

Rebecca narrowed her eyes as she glanced at me. 'A body!'

'What?'

'The body of a man who's been dead a long time.'

'Shut up, Rebecca!' Jonah snapped.

'How did he die?' I thought of her knife. Of what she'd told me in the dunes. I glanced at Jonah.

'Don't listen to her.'

'Do you want to see the body, Fishgirl?'

Jonah turned sharply. 'I said, shut up, Rebecca! You haven't seen the body! No one's going to see it! Don't spoil this!'

I glanced at him. His face was smeared and dabbed with white and black clay again. He seemed strange. Nervous.

'What about the body? Who is he?'

Rebecca laughed. 'Be patient, Fishgirl. Just do what we say.'

'What if I don't want to?'

'You don't get to choose.'

'Stop that, Rebecca!' Jonah snapped. 'Don't fool around. I told you, everything has to be right for it to happen. If you fool around it won't work!'

I looked from one to the other. 'For what to happen? And what won't work?'

Jonah looked back at me. 'It's like this. First we're going to sit quietly. Then I'm going to play music. Then we're going on a journey. To a place you've never been to before.'

'Where?'

Rebecca grinned. 'Just be patient!'

Jonah lit a few more candles and placed them in a

circle. The long, drawn-out figures in the paintings bent stiffly and jumped and danced in the flickering light. Boskind came closer and sat down. He looked around at us with the dark, watchful eyes of a small bushbuck.

I glanced at Jonah and Rebecca passing the cigarette in silence between each other. My skin felt prickly. Suddenly, the cave seemed hot. I thought of the layers and layers of rock piled up high over my head. Pressing down and crushing the breath out of me. The silence was so thick I heard the sound of my heart thumping in my ears. 'What're we waiting for?' I whispered.

'You can't hurry things.' Jonah reached for the long musical bow he had played before. He tested the taut gut with his thumb. A gentle twang filled the cave and echoed against the walls. Then he took a fierce draw on a fresh cigarette Rebecca had rolled. He looked across at me. In the candlelight I caught the sharp glint of cheetah eyes. In contrast, Rebecca's eyes were dark and hooded. Mysterious shadows fell over her face in the candlelight.

Then Jonah picked up a stick. This time, he held the upper part of the bow against his left shoulder. The lower end he rested against a large, hollow gourd on the sand. He tapped softly against the gut with the stick. It started to quiver and hum. Every now and again he put his chin against the string to stop the vibration.

The sounds came out long and sad. They echoed inside the hollow of the gourd. It was a very different kind of music to what he'd played before. It wove through the air, filling the space of the cave, sending shivers down my spine.

Next to me the small boy started clapping. A slow heartbeat to the bow music.

Smoke drifted in the candlelight. The faces around me became hazy. Shapes softened. I blinked. Perhaps I was falling asleep. The music spread out and wrapped itself around me. I was caught in a giant web of music.

It fell down over my shoulders. Trapped me. Melted my bones.

Around the cave, the paintings of men with stick legs and antelope heads seemed strange. They swayed and moved to the music. The long arms and legs were swimming rather than running. Swimming in circles above our shoulders. The rock was starting to gleam. Everything was turning transparent. Layer upon layer of people and animals were coming up through the rock towards us. Floating right out into the circle of candlelight. Surrounding us. Dancing and chanting and circling to the music. Surrounding us with webs of yellow thread.

The cave wall had grown soft and vaporous. I reached out to touch it. But there was nothing there. It had gone. The rock had disappeared. The cave didn't exist anymore. There was nothing but a soft velvet feel to the air.

Luminous zigzags and lines flickered in front of me. Moved and leaped to the beat of the music. Far in the distance was a dark place. It seemed to be drawing me. Drawing me on like a tunnel. I looked around at the others but they'd disappeared.

There was only music filling the space.

Music and the feeling of my body changing.

'It's time to go.' It was Jonah's voice.

I turned to look at where the voice had come from. Out of the darkness a cheetah stared back at me. Eyes reflecting amber. Sleek shoulders spotted with black and gold. High, honeyed cheekbones ridged with black. Mouth open and panting. Lips curled back to reveal sharp white teeth.

Everything else had faded away. Rebecca, the boy and the cave – they had all gone. I was alone. Facing this wild animal with fear beating behind my eyes.

A deep growl came from the cheetah's throat. 'We

must go.'

I sensed dark markings on my own face. Shadows at my eyes. Long lines down my nose. I felt the heaviness of the horns as I stood up and stretched my neck.

'Come!' The sound was more a pant than a word.

I understood. I stepped forward. Felt the strange weight of my flanks. Felt the strength of my legs under me. I flicked my head from side to side. Snorted the dust from my nostrils. A dizziness filled my head. The earth seemed to reel. Then the sky turned inky blue like lapis lazuli. Stars and galaxies rushed across it.

I look down at my body. I'm truly a gemsbok. Standing on a vast plain against a dark, luminous sky.

17

People of the Plain

In the distance, shapes of people advance towards us along the skyline.

'Who are they, Jonah?' I whisper.

'The First People. My ancestors.'

'Why're we here?'

'I'm not sure.'

I snort air from my nostrils. 'You *must* know! This is *your* place, not mine! They're *your* ancestors, Jonah!'

He glances at me, then growls. 'I'm not Jonah. I'm Cheetah.'

'Yes . . . but . . .'

'This is the place we all come from. Watch and listen. Something will be shown to us.'

'Yes . . . but . . .'

'You're an antelope-girl now. You hold the stars between your horns. Your name is Spirit of the Desert.'

'I don't want to be Spirit of the Desert! Or an antelope-girl! I want to be myself. I want to go back to where I belong.'

'You can't.' His voice rasps from the back of his throat.

'Never—?'

'Not now. Not yet.'

'Why not?'

'You must draw on their spirit-power.'

'Why?'

'To find your own power. You have to be healed.'

'I'm not sick! This is stupid. It makes no sense!' I know what Vanessa would say. But Vanessa has been left behind in another world. 'Jonah, I'm Fish! Not an antelope-girl! Or anything else!'

Jonah stands with his shoulders hunched forward and his head held low. He looks at me through narrow yellow eyes, his pupils dark black slits in the strange light. Behind the eyes is a fierce anger. I sense he's about to leap. To spring at me and tear at my throat. Rip out my heart. That's what cheetahs do. They hunt antelope.

But all he says is, 'You have to believe.'

'Believe what?'

'Believe in yourself and who you are.'

I stamp my foot. A puff of pale dry dust rises. 'I don't know who I am. Don't you see? I'm confused. I have to go back. I don't want to be here.'

'You can't go back. It's too late. They're coming towards us.'

The people are in front of us now. They stand gathered in a circle around a fire. The sky has darkened and is turning milky with stars. Against the darkness, a thorn tree traps the moon in a net of branches. They're singing. Soft sounds that melt into the night.

They're small with amber eyes and skin the colour of pale, creamed honey. They wear feathers and beads in their hair and bracelets of ostrich shells and cowries on their arms. On their ankles are bracelets of small cocoon-rattles. Softened skins are tied around their hips. They move with lightness. As if their legs and arms float. The seeds inside the cocoon-rattles make a soft *shirr-shirr* music as they move.

They settle on the ground in a circle around the fire, speaking with soft clicking sounds in the back of their throats. A sound of pebbles tumbling in a stream. Or raindrops thudding against dry earth.

'What're they saying?' I whisper.

'They're talking of a hunt. They know we're here.'

'Shouldn't we run?

He shakes his head. 'Listen!'

'But they've arrows. And we're animals. Won't they hunt us?'

'No! They know we're *spirit*-animals. That we've come to them in dreams. Just listen. They're telling their story. Inviting us to listen.'

'Why?'

'They're offering us their *!gi*.' He says the sound with a sharp click.

'What does *!gi* mean?' I struggle to say it the same way.

'Spirit-power.'

'What're they telling?'

'Stop talking! Just listen!' His voice rasps with impatience. 'If you don't stay silent, how'll you ever hear? Listen with your heart. When they see you're listening, they'll know you're part of the moment.'

On the other side of the fire a man is speaking. The sound of his voice makes a pattern. He tells a story. Every now and again one of the others adds a few words.

I hold my head high. Force my ears to catch the strange click sounds. Words rise up from the circle. Like sparks from the fire. It's the story of a hunt. Long, long ago.

'There was a man. He had a friend. And this man said to his friend, Brother, there is an ostrich in the bush.'

The man telling the story flaps his arms and stalks around the people at the fire. He makes angry ostrich movements. The seeds inside the cocoon-rattles *shirr . . . shirr* restlessly as he strides about.

'The ostrich has made his nest. We must hunt this ostrich. We must shoot it with our arrows. The poison will make it lie down. When it dies we will pluck it of its feathers and strip it of its black skin.'

The man's hands weave and slice through the firelight. Plucking and stripping. His story becomes a dance. He speaks faster and faster.

'We will cut out the liver and make a fire and roast the liver on hot stones. The liver will make us strong. We will cut up the meat and put it in a net made of twisted bark. We will tie the net with sticks and put a strong stick through the net to carry it home to our wives.

123

We will take the bones so the children may suck the marrow.'

Across the fire, a woman answers,

'The wives will say, The thigh meat we will hang on bushes to dry. Some meat we will roast and eat as soon as it has cooled. Some we will slice and cook in a pot of water. When the liquid fat comes to the top we will collect it in the breastbone of the ostrich and dip the cooked meat into these juices.'

The first storyteller jumps in again. The words click sharply in his mouth, like pebbles rattling in a tin.

'I did not mean to shoot our brother. I was shooting my arrow at the ostrich. Our brother jumped in front of me. He did not see it. He was looking at the ostrich. I weep. For I have shot my brother.'

From the circle another voice speaks. His words are fireflies darting into the night.

'Do not weep, my friends. I was not watching. The arrow came between the dust. The ostrich ran between us. The wound is serious but you must speak gently to the man who shot me. It was the arrow's fault. My brother did not shoot me. The arrow shot me. I know that I shall die. For the wound is large. The poison strong. Lift me up. Carry me. My wife, fetch firewood to make a fire. For I shall not sleep tonight. Make the fire well so the cold will not kill the children. I shall not see you again. The time of talk is over. My heart is falling.'

Around the fire the people nod.

'His heart is falling.'

The first man stands up again.

'My brother, your friends will help. We will lift you onto a kaross. We will wrap you in the kaross.'

The man scoops armfuls of night air as he wraps an invisible cloak over the friend.

'When day breaks we will find a place of soft earth to bury you. We will lay stones over the place so the hyena will not dig you out.'

And the man packs stones in a heap in the air. Now the woman speaks. Her voice is soft. I strain to catch the words.

'My heart stands over my husband. He ran well, hunting the ostrich. He dies before he has grown a beard. He dies while he is still young. My heart trembles. My house stands cold. I have no man to fetch the wood. My fire has gone out.'

The voices around the fire sigh.

'You must go to your father. You must take your children. You must not sit here by your husband's grave. You will grow sick.'

The woman looks around the group.

'The path to my father is difficult. There are wild animals. Who will go with me? Who will fight the wild animals for me?'

126

A chorus of voices answers like crickets chirping.

> *'We cannot go. The waterholes at which we
> live are our father's waterholes. We grew up
> living by them. It is our father's father's water.
> Our grandfather's father walked this place and
> so it is our place. If we leave, others will come
> and take this land from us. We cannot go.'*

The story stops. They look at the woman. Then she
speaks quietly.

> *'My heart is trembling. For hunger is not soft.
> We do not hunger gently.'*

An old woman stands. Touches the woman's face.
She hangs a skin stitched with ostrich feathers around
the woman's shoulders and ties a skin *kaross* around
her hips.

> *'You must take a digging stick to search for
> roots. We will give you dried meat and ostrich
> shells filled with water and a honey-bag so
> your children may eat the liquid fat of the
> honey on the journey.'*

127

The other woman asks,

'How will I find the way?'

The hot ash of her words burns pinpricks along my spine. The man looks directly at me. I stare back. Then he speaks.

'The stars and the spirits will guide you.'

I hold his look. See the reflection in his eyes. The dark 'V'-shadow of gemsbok horns shows in them.

Suddenly, the faces dissolve in the firelight. The sky reels overhead.

We're no longer under a deep blue lapis lazuli sky. We're in blinding sunlight. In the middle of a dry empty plain. A yellow plain stretching to the far horizon, under a white sky with a hot sun beating down. The people have disappeared. There's no sign of them. All that remains is a small circle of charred earth and a patch of dry, grey ash on the ground. Some wisps of ostrich feather float in the air.

I swing around to face Jonah. 'What? What now?'

'We must go with her.'

'We can't. We don't know this place. It might be dangerous.'

'It's too late for that. I told you we were going on a journey.'

'But . . .?' But Jonah is already far in the distance with his body slung low between the yellow grass. Ahead of him is the woman. She walks with a baby slung in a skin across her breast, another clinging to her back and another child walking alongside her, holding tightly to the *kaross* draped across her hips.

'Wait, Jonah! We must go back. We have to go home.' I look over my shoulder. Where *is* back? And where *is* home? In which direction? How long have we been gone? Will my father find me if we don't return?

I hear Vanessa's voice. So, you think you can just run off into the wild?

This is not me, Vanessa!

If it's not you, who is it?

I stamp my foot. I'm an antelope. Don't you see, Vanessa? A gemsbok.

Rubbish! It's your imagination, Fish. You've got too much imagination. You *can't* be a gemsbok.

But I feel like one. I sense the markings on my face. I feel the weight of the horns. I feel the power of my body. I know this plain. I know where the woman has to go to. I see the place she has to reach. It's a long journey into the Red Desert. There are lions along the way and very little water.

So now you have x-ray eyes! Who said anything about the Red Desert?

I just know this. We have to go with her. We have to protect her on a journey back to her people.

What do you know about protecting anyone, Fish?

What d'you mean?

When you could've saved your mother, did you? Did you, Fish?

Words! Words! Words! Always words with Vanessa!

Jonah is far ahead. There's nothing to do but follow.

Dust catches my nostrils. Sweat prickles my skin. When the sun beats at its fiercest, a dark shape forms in the corner of my eye. There seems to be a shadow slinking behind us. Something stalking.

Vanessa? Is that you following us? Stop playing games.

'Do you see it, Jonah?' I whisper.

'What?'

'Someone's following us.'

'There's nothing.'

'There is! It's behind us all the time.'

Jonah stops. He stands with his neck stretched high

above the grass, his nose twitching. His eyes blaze across the dry plain. 'There's nothing.'

'There is! When I move, it moves. When I stop, it stops.'

'It's the shadow of the sun going behind a cloud. Or an eagle's shadow as it flies overhead.'

'No!' I snort. 'It's something more than an eagle's shadow. I feel it. Do you think my eyes see differently now that I'm an antelope?'

But my eyes *do* see differently. I watch Jonah flick his head and then stop to gnaw the front of his paw. And as he does so, I see the rough pads underneath. Pads like those underneath a dog's paw. Each pad thick and cracked and, at the edge of each toe, long claws as sharp as knives.

Finally, the woman rests in the shade of a thorn tree. She spreads out her *kaross*. Unties the sling which holds her baby. She hangs a small meat sling high in a branch. Then she takes an ostrich egg from a net of plaited grass. She pulls out the plug of grass that stops the small drinking hole and holds the ostrich egg up for each child to sip.

They sit and wait for the sun to lose its sting. In the distance a single rock makes a sharp needle into the sky. Above it is a falcon. It flies in wide circles, tilting its wings on the hot thermal air currents. A small bird darts just below.

Jonah rests on a termite mound at the edge of a dry river bed, with his head held high. I watch him inspect the terrain. Since when has his face become so strong? He looks like a sphinx staring out over the desert.

I raise my head. Put out my tongue to taste the air. My nostrils flare as they sense something. A strange smell. Not just dry bush. Not just the small mauve flowers on the thorn tree. But something else. A heavy sickly smell. A hideous smell. Of old blood. Rotting meat.

Jonah has picked it up as well. He stands. Gives a low grunt. The hair at his neck prickles.

'See!' I tell him. 'You feel it too! There's something out there!'

'Yes . . .' He growls from the back of his throat.

Suddenly a ragged dog-like creature appears in the bend of the dry river bed. Its fur is matted and tufted in different colours of black and brown. Its ears upright. Its jaws hanging open, vicious teeth showing. It stands silent as a shadow next to the trunk of a dead tree, and stares at the woman.

The skin along my back prickles. 'What is it? A wild dog?'

'No! Worse. A hyena.'

The woman has seen it as well. She grabs her three children. In silence they watch. Then the hyena snuffles nearer, its nose quivering along the tracks in the dry sand. She picks up a handful of sand and throws it. The hyena draws back its head and whoops a blood-curdling sound.

Jonah curls his lip and growls.

'Does it know we're here?'

He shakes his head. 'It doesn't see us. We're spirit-animals. But it senses something. That's why it's keeping its distance for a while.'

'Can't we chase it off?'

'No. Right now we're invisible. But keep still. Don't show yourself. A cheetah and an antelope are no match for a hyena. One bite from those jaws and our necks will be broken.'

'Surely we must run for it?'

'Don't run!' he snarls.

I look at him sharply. Cheetahs are the fastest animal on earth. They can outrun anything. He could easily outrun the hyena. He's staying not only to protect the woman and her children, but to protect me.

The hyena sniffs the air. It catches the scent of the

ST. ALOYSIUS COLLEGE LIBRARY

sling filled with dried meat hanging in the tree. It pads forward. So close now I smell the rotting meat stink of its breath. It stops a few paces from the woman. She sits, frozen.

It stands up on its hind legs. Tears the sling from the branch. Drags it a short distance away. With a fierce rip it pulls the skin apart and gulps the meat down. Then it lies down panting in the hot sun. Huge, jagged teeth showing through the bloodied muzzle.

Silence. Just the sound of a small bird rustling in the thorn tree. High against the white sky the raptor circles. A vulture, perhaps? Waiting to swoop in after the kill?

The woman sits watching the hyena watch her. She has to make a choice. Which child must she hold? She clutches the smallest child and holds the digging stick as a weapon in her other hand.

Soon darkness will come. And then?

18

Home

My father handed me a mug of soup straight from the stove. I cradled my hands around it. Closed my eyes. Breathed in the normal tomato-vegetable smell. Listened to the sound of the sea beating below Rockwood. And waited for my heart to still.

My body was numb. Tired, as if I'd swum all the way to the Antarctic. How long was it to real moonrise? Only at *real* moonrise would I know if there was truly a sickle moon.

Jonah had stood with the light of the setting sun colouring his face. We've done what we had to do, he'd said. When the sickle moon comes she'll be fine. We must return now.

The sickle moon? Why?

But he hadn't waited to answer. He'd padded off across the plain. Running east, away from the sunset towards the night.

I ran after him into the dusk. A wind blowing bitter against my face and stinging my nostrils as I raced to keep up. My legs soon aching and numb. In the darkness the stars drilled icy holes into the cold metal of a steel sky.

Then I was back in the cave. Shaking with cold. Feeling the rocks crowd in on me. Ice in my bones. We all were there in the cave. All four of us. Rebecca, Boskind, Jonah and I. Yet none of us spoke. We sat shivering. Our eyes wide. Looking at each other in the candlelight. Searching each others eyes for answers to the things we had seen. Squinting into the darkness over our shoulders beyond the candles. Searching the paintings on the rock for clues. Feeling the coldness of the night at our backs. Hoping for some warmth to return to our bodies.

Afterwards, I'd hurried home to Rockwood. To its windows sending patches of light over the wet sand. To the stone tower with its shell lining. To its warmth. And now I clutched my mug of soup and eyed my father. 'Is there a place called the Red Desert?'

'Some call it that, but it's really the Kalahari Desert, where the sand is more orange than red. It's where I went when I was doing my research.'

'What's it like?'

'Dry. Hot. Waterless. A few scraggly thorn trees. A scorching wind. Blazing hot during the day. Bitterly cold at night.'

'How can anyone survive, if there's no water?'

'Some do. By finding melons that store water. Unearthing roots and tubers. Collecting dew when it falls. Digging for a muddy trickle under the ground. Why're you asking?' He searched my face.

I shrugged. 'It sounds a frightening place.'

He blew over the surface of his soup. Took a small sip. 'Frightening?' Then he shook his head. 'No. Nothing is frightening when you know what's expected of you.'

Even though the soup was hot I felt a shiver go through me. What would be expected of me if I went to the Red Desert?

He eyed me over the rim of his mug. 'What's troubling you, Fish?'

I searched his face. How could I explain about today's journey?

'Well?'

I shrugged. It was hard. I tried to find a place to begin. 'Is there some way to get between this world and another? Like a bridge?'

'Hmm . . . that's a tough one. I'm not an engineer.'

'Stop teasing. I don't mean a steel girder and cement kind of bridge. Another type.'

'Another type?' He tilted back on his chair. Drummed his fingers against the table. 'That's a question with a complicated answer.'

'So . . .?'

'You can bridge two worlds in your imagination by putting yourself in the place of someone else. By feeling what they feel.'

'I mean, more than that. By physically going.'

'It's not a physical crossing between one world and another, it's more spiritual. We can be joined spiritually in many experiences.'

'How?'

'There are two parts to all of us. The spiritual and the physical. The spiritual is the wiser part.'

'How does that help?'

'Well, for instance, the spiritual me knows there is no such thing as death. The spiritual me knows death comes to our body but not to our spirit. That the life we live after death is longer than the life we live here in this world.'

'That's difficult to understand.'

'Yes, because we get muddled. We believe everything that happens to us now is the only world. We forget about our spirit. But if you're in tune with your spirit you can move freely between worlds.'

'So what's the bridge, then?' I scooped up the last smidgens of soup with my finger and licked it.

'There's no real bridge, because there's no real gap. The physical and spiritual are one in all of us. You can move from one world to another by being in tune with both. You have to find the spiritual energy that connects you.'

'Does Jonah have it?'

'Hmmm . . . perhaps. Maybe sometimes.'

And me? I wanted to ask. What about me? But I already knew the answer. When I painted, all my worlds came together. My hand followed my heart. I could forget everything. Forget there'd been a storm. That the boat had overturned. Forget that Mum had gone. Forget this huge dark space that swirled around me. Forget the words going around and around in my head. And the feeling of being caught somewhere. Trapped.

I couldn't tell Vanessa about the two worlds and what my father had said. She wouldn't have wanted to hear it. But later I went up the cliff-path and told her about the journey.

I suppose you're going to say you attacked the

hyena, saved the woman and her children, and went back to the cave a hero, she said.

How could I have done that? A cheetah and a gemsbok wouldn't stand a chance against the jaws of a hyena. In any case, we were invisible to it.

Invisible?

Yes. As long as we stood still we were invisible. We stayed like that for a long while. The woman, the children, the two of us and the hyena. Each keeping our distance. Then as the sun began to set, the hyena stood up. Slunk in closer.

And then?

That's when the bird attacked.

The vulture that'd been circling?

Except it wasn't a vulture. It was an eagle. It fell like a stone from the sky. It plummeted down onto the hyena.

Eagles don't attack hyenas.

This one did. It stuck its claws into the hyena's shoulders. Huge black talons ripped into it.

It must've had a nest in the thorn tree it was protecting.

I shook my head. No, there wasn't a nest.

What, then?

Nothing. Just a small swallow sitting on a branch.

So you're telling me the hyena was about to attack the woman when an eagle drove it away?

I took a deep breath. In a way.

Vanessa narrowed her eyes. What do you mean – in a way?

Well it didn't just drive it away. It killed the hyena.

Killed? An eagle killed the hyena?

Yes.

Rubbish! You're making this up. It's another one of your imaginary stories. The whole thing is made up. First you become an antelope, then you step through a rock wall into another world! Then you listen to the stories of people who've been long gone dead, speaking a language you've never heard before! And you understand their stories! Then you believe you have to protect a woman who's being attacked by a hyena! Then an eagle drops out of the sky like magic and kills the hyena! And you want me to *believe* you?

Silence. It's hard to argue with Vanessa.

Don't you see, Fish? Your story's completely made up. It's another one of your imaginary things. It's all lies! You have to stop this.

It's not lies! Jonah said it was happening for a reason. That I was being given some sort of power. That his ancestors were offering me their power.

Power to do what?

Power to . . . I couldn't answer Vanessa. It was too complicated. We were both silent for a while, staring at each other.

Then she sighed. OK . . . go on!

Jonah said there'd be a new moon.

A new moon? What's that got to do with it?

Jonah says a new moon is a good moon. A curved moon carries things carefully. It would carry the woman to safety.

That's ridiculous! The moon can't carry something! Least of all a woman!

Silence.

So the hyena died, the woman walked off, and you went back to the cave where Rebecca and the small boy were waiting for you?

No. Rebecca and Boskind were out on the plain with us.

What? Why didn't you tell me that before!

I didn't know until afterwards.

What do you mean?

Boskind was the swallow trying to distract the hyena.

And Rebecca?

Rebecca was the eagle.

What? Rebecca? The eagle? That's ridiculous!

I nodded. You said she was dangerous. And she was. I didn't know it was her. She flew high and silently above us when we followed the woman.

Do you expect me to believe Rebecca can fly? *Fly?* Vanessa snapped her fingers. Just like that?

I nodded again. She did. She swooped down. She had enormous talons. She tore into the hyena. She picked him up. And flew up again. I felt the breeze of her wings against my face. She soared up as if she'd never done anything else but fly. As if she'd always known such a wide open space as the sky. You should've seen her. She was strong. Powerful. It was incredible to watch.

An eagle isn't strong enough to pick up a hyena!

Rebecca was. She was stronger than any bird I've seen. Her wings were huge. I was terrified of her. She flew in at incredible speed and snatched up the hyena in her claws in front of us.

What did this eagle look like?

Brown with a speckled white chest. Huge white legs. Also speckled. It was massive. With its wings stretched out, from tip to tip, probably about six feet.

Six feet! Impossible. No eagle's that size.

Rebecca wasn't an ordinary eagle. She was a martial eagle – the biggest in Africa. I found a picture of one in a book.

How do you know it was Rebecca?

I just *knew*. She perched on the thorn tree with her shoulders hunched, the rusty crown on her head standing up, and challenged us with her eyes. Eyes that were hooded, piercing and terrifying. Like the eyes in the book. Like Rebecca's eyes.

She . . .? She did this? *She* did that? Stop this, Fish! It wasn't a *she*. It was a *bird*! Rebecca's not an eagle!

I know it was her. I knew it after she dropped the hyena.

Dropped?

I nodded. She dropped it right onto the needle rock sticking up into the sky. She dropped him as easily as an eagle drops a snake to break its backbone. She killed the hyena. So the woman is safe.

For once Vanessa seemed not to find any words. In silence I challenged her to argue. But I knew better! Across the sea I watched the new moon rising. Jonah was right. It came up thin and curved. A tilted, sickle moon. It would carry the woman and her children safely on.

19

The Thoughts of the Boy who Follows the Girl

I am the silent swallow. I fly in circles high above the earth. It spreads out beneath me. Pale and silent in the scorching sun. Everything below is small. The dry thorn trees make tiny curls of shade like ash against the earth. Seven dots move across the earth. Four in front. Two behind. The seventh even further. Like tiny ants they crawl across the sand.

Finally they stop. From above I watch the last shadow slink in closer. I fly down. I have to distract this shadow. I flit from branch to branch, rustling the dry leaves. Unable to sing. Unable to attack. I'm too small. I'm not as strong as my sister.

She flies higher in a fury of ruffled feathers. Her wings spread wide. Her head twists sharply as she searches the ground below, her tail-feathers streaming, her talons tucked under. She is the strongest of all birds. She's not silent. She screeches her clear call of *klee . . . klee . . . kloee . . . kloeee . . . !*

My sister hovers. For a moment her shape blocks out the sun. Then she falls like a stone from the sky. Her talons out. She rakes the creature. Claws it up and drops him. She drops him on the hard sharp stone and shatters his strength.

This creature – this hyena – can no longer harm us. She kills him.

All this I've seen and cannot tell. My sister has killed the spirit of my father. She is free. I watch her soar upwards. Fly high against the sun.

I am the silent swallow. I follow the girl. She doesn't hear me. I follow her up the cliff-path. Past the church. Through the graveyard. We come to the green cave that is not a true cave but a huge tree growing in the middle of the graveyard, with branches scraping the ground.

This time I don't wait at the edge, I follow her right inside.

She takes some matches from her pocket. She strikes one. I see the sand is decorated with shells laid out in patterns. Rows of creamy round ones. Rows of pink and purple flat ones. The last row is of big knobbly *arikreukels* as big as my fist. There are small stubs of candles inside each *arikreukel* shell. She lights them. Strikes more matches to get them all lit. They make a circle of light around her.

A plank of wood is stuck into the ground. There're letters on it. Just one word. Two 'S's and two 'A's and an 'E'. I know these letters from my name. But I don't know this word.

She sits quietly inside the circle of light. After a while she begins to speak. She doesn't talk to me. She hasn't seen me. She speaks towards the plank of wood.

I sit still and listen.

She whispers the words. Her lips hardly move.

I get up quietly and put my ear against a branch of the tree. It tells me it's very old. It tells me there're insects living under its bark. But this isn't what I'm listening for.

I put my ear against the ground. The earth tells me the sea is hammering far below at the bottom of the cliff. But this isn't what I'm listening for either. I'm listening for something else. Listening for the person she's talking to.

But there's nothing. Just the plank of wood. And the circle of candles. Truly there is nothing. It's a mystery.

20

The Forfeit

We walked high along the edge of Whale Rock cliff, Jonah and I. Far below, a colony of seals was basking on the rocks. Waddling about on their flippers and barking at each other. Then slipping back into the smooth swells without a splash. Black and shiny like blobs of grease in the sunlight.

We walked, one behind the other, along the narrow path, the seagulls gliding low over our heads, the sun glittering on the sea and the smell of sea spray mingling with the smell of *fynbos* clinging to the cliffs.

Neither of us spoke. It was as if the magic would break if we said anything about what had happened at the cave.

At the end point where the path dipped down to the fishermen's hut on the rock ledge below, the sea was wilder. It swept around on every side. Plunging, soaring and crashing against the rocks. A wide, ragged place, with rocks worn sharp like razors and cormorants screeching.

I hugged the sea smell to my chest. 'You can see all the way to the Antarctic from here!'

'You can't!'

I smiled at Jonah. 'But you can pretend.'

'When the north-wester blows, the spray shoots as high as the cliffs. It's dangerous on the fishing ledge, then. You can be swept off. And there's no way of getting up again.'

I glanced back at him. 'Is this where you fished with your father?'

He nodded. 'My ancestors fished here as well. They made rock-pool traps here. Built stone walls across the deep gullies. At high tide the fish washed in – especially on moonless nights when it was dark. When the tide went out again, the fish were trapped. It was easy to catch them in nets then.'

'I thought your ancestors were hunters, not fisher-men.'

'They were both. They moved from place to place. When they lived next to the sea, they ate fish and mussels. After it rained and the plants began growing and the animals returned to the plains, they moved back and hunted again. Pa says the sea was far from here once.' He pointed towards the horizon. 'This was all land. When the ice melted, the sea came back.'

I squinted into the distance, trying to imagine the dark blue sea as land. Suddenly a fine, white spray shot up just beyond the edge of the rock.

'A whale!'

We shaded our eyes and scanned the rolling water. There were five of them just beyond the white foam at the edge of the cliff. We climbed down to the ledge – so close we could hear the hollow rumbling of air passing through their blowholes and the hiss of breath as they came up and snorted. They rolled and heaved through the water, bumping and nudging each other.

'They know we're here.'

Jonah looked at me. 'How?'

'They're calling us. Listen.'

He shook his head. 'We're not spirit-animals now.'

'I know. But it's the same. The whales are calling our spirits.'

'To do what?' I felt Jonah's eyes on me.

I shrugged. 'Just to be here this moment. They know we're listening. That we're part of their world.'

As if in answer, a whale lifted its tail. It hit its flukes

hard against the water. The sound echoed up against the cliff. Then there was a shout.

'Hey! You two!'

I turned. It was Rebecca. She was standing on the edge of the cliff above us. Leaning out. Her hair catching the sun. Her body, like a carved wooden masthead on an old sailing ship, leaning out to catch the wind and spray.

I didn't call back. Nor did Jonah. Rebecca had broken the magic spell.

'Hey – you two!' The crashing sea carried her voice away. 'I've a plan.'

'What?' Jonah shouted back at her.

'It's time for the forfeit.'

'What forfeit?'

'Fishgirl knows. I showed her the house in the dunes. She has to repay me.'

Jonah caught my look and shook his head. 'She doesn't owe you anything!'

'Hah! That's what you say. But I know differently. A forfeit is a forfeit. I've come to collect it.'

I looked back at her looming above us with the sun at her back. Today she had on her armour. Her claws were out. She was Rebecca the martial eagle. Rebecca the Valkyrie. She was a Valkyrie about to fly over her battlefield.

151

A shiver went down my spine as I watched her climb down the path towards us.

'So, Fishgirl . . .' Her eyes flashed. 'You have to show us why you're called Fish.'

I stared back at her. 'Why?'

'Because I say so.'

Jonah clicked his tongue. 'That's not an answer, Rebecca. Stop playing games.'

'Stay out of this, Jonah! She has to prove herself.' Then she narrowed her eyes. '*I* have.'

'That was different, Rebecca. You know that!'

I eyed her. 'What do you want?'

'I dare you to jump into the sea from here and swim. Like you say you can. Swim in the sea. If you're a fish, that's what fish do. You wouldn't do it the other night from the beach. So jump in now. I dare you! Show us you can swim.'

'I *can* swim.'

'I've never seen you.'

'So?'

'Prove it!'

'She doesn't have to, Rebecca.'

'You stay out of this, Jonah. This is for Fishgirl. Fish swim. She's the one who has to prove it. '

'I don't.'

152

'Too scared?'

'I'm not.'

'Do it, then!'

I turned to look at the sea. The whales had disappeared. But the swells were still rolling in. Throwing themselves against the rock ledge and hissing back again in a swirling mass of foam. I could! I could swim in this sea off this point! I had done it before. Swum and swum. I had swum all the way back to the beach that time.

But I couldn't save her.

'Don't do it, Fish! You won't be able to get back out again. You'll be cut to pieces against the rocks. You don't have to listen to Rebecca. You don't have to prove anything.'

The sea was roaring in my head. We stared from one to another.

Then Rebecca spoke. 'You know you have to, Fish. A forfeit's a forfeit.'

She took a step towards me. Held my eyes. For a moment I felt she might push me backwards off the ledge. One hard shove was all it would take.

I was already falling. Falling down, down, down into darkness.

Her eyes flicked across my face. 'Hah! That's what I thought! You're too scared!'

Silence. A cormorant shrieked. I bit my lip.

Jonah stepped between us and faced Rebecca. 'No!'

'What d'you mean, *no*?'

'She can't swim here. You know what happened here with my father!'

'So where?' Rebecca's eyes suddenly brightened. 'I know!'

'Where?'

'The Hole. The one in the ledge on the other side of the Point. I dare you. I dare you to swim to the bottom of the Hole.'

Jonah shook his head. 'No! Not there, either.'

I glanced across at Jonah. 'I can do it.'

Jonah eyed me. 'Have you seen the Hole?'

I shook my head.

'Then decide after you've seen it.'

'No. She either accepts now, or she has to swim here. Which is it?'

'I'll swim to the bottom of the Hole.'

'Good, then.'

When we stopped at the edge of the Hole, I knew why Jonah had asked if I'd seen it. It lay in the rock shelf, a deep dark unblinking eye completely over-shadowed by the cliff, worn into the rock by swirling waves. The water as dark as poison. As black as tombstone marble. There was no way of knowing how deep it went. Or what was below the smooth, oily surface.

Rebecca shot a look at me. 'They say there's a giant octopus trapped in there. Washed in. Never washed out. Just grew bigger and bigger. They say it hides deep down, waiting for food.'

'That's a lie, Rebecca!'

'How do you know, Jonah? You've never dived down. The octopus squirts ink. Blinds you. That's why the water's so dark.'

'You don't have to do this, Fish!'

'Go on, Fishgirl! And bring back a pebble or a shell from the bottom to prove you've been all the way down.'

I stood at the lip of rock and looked at the inky blackness. Tried to peer into the deep, dark eye. The poison-black water. But the shiny tombstone surface reflected nothing but my outline against the cliffs.

I pulled off my shoes. Stood poised with my feet at the edge. Then took a deep breath. Closed my eyes. Stepped off. Let my body fall straight down feet first into the icy blackness.

Down, down, down. Black pressing against my eyelids. No sound. No whales calling *Fishhh . . . Fishhh . . . Fishhh . . .* Just silence.

ST. ALOYSIUS COLLEGE LIBRARY

Then I turned. Kicked. And began to swim to the bottom. Down, down, down. There was no end to it. No bottom. Just deep, icy darkness that went on for ever. And the slithering feel of seaweed – or was it a tentacle touching my skin? Reaching for me. I could feel the tentacles. Feel them coming towards me. Huge suckers on the end of them, searching for me.

My hand touched something. Something hard and rough. Shells? Stones? Rock? I grabbed. Turned. Kicked as hard as I could. Swam upwards. Towards light bouncing through the water. My lungs burning. My head exploding. Light shattering. Someone grabbing my arms. I gasped and pulled air into my lungs.

'Did you get it? Give it to me!'

The two of them were bending over me. Their faces swimming in the sunlight.

'She's got nothing! She didn't touch the bottom!'

I heaved on my arms and dragged my legs over the slippery edge. Lay down on the warm rock with water streaming from every part of me.

'Where's the rock or shell she's supposed to have brought back?'

I opened my clenched fist. Too tired to speak. There in the palm of my hand I had a spotted pebble. Except it wasn't a pebble. It was a small cowrie shell with a pattern like Chinese writing.

'See, Rebecca. She's got it.'

'Hah! She probably took it down with her. She had it all the time. Jumped in with it in her hand.'

'Except she didn't. You know it, Rebecca! She went right to the bottom. She's paid her forfeit!'

21

Star Song

Jonah held the candle higher. I stared down at the man lying peacefully like an Egyptian mummy half-buried in the sand. His skin shrunken against his bones. A creamy ostrich-shell necklace around his neck. He was hidden under a shelf of rock, surrounded by the paintings of eland and dancing people.

'Who is he?' I whispered.

'Heart Fire. Named after the Day Star which appears in the sky every morning just before the sun. His spirit is the fire that brings warmth to our hearts.'

'Does anyone know he's here?'

'You mean, like grave-robbers? People who steal away the mysteries of the ancestors? Who rob the ancestors of their spirit?'

I nodded.

Jonah shook his head. 'You're the only other person,

apart from Pa, who's seen him. His spirit mustn't be disturbed.'

Suddenly I thought of another body. Sara Baartman's. Whose bones had hung on a stand inside a glass case in a museum far, far away. Whose brains and organs had been put in two bottles. What about *her* spirit? And what about all the others before her? And all the others after her whose bones were lying in drawers in museums? Sara Baartman and all of the people who had been robbed of their spirit – what about *them*?

I looked down at the man lying peacefully in the sand and then back at Jonah. 'What about the others?'

'Who?'

'Every person whose bones have been disturbed. What about Sara Baartman?'

'Who's she?'

'She came home in a box. Just a box of bones and some bottles with her insides floating in them.'

'From where?'

'From a museum. Where they keep bones of people they think are strange and interesting. They show them in glass cases. Sometimes they preserve just the heads. The head is chopped off the body and the skin from the neck is wrapped under the jaw. And at the back of the scalp are stitches where the skull has been cut open to take out the brains. They put glass eyes into the eye sockets. Sometimes the hair falls out and their faces shrink. My father's seen numbers painted in ink on their foreheads, like GX 73.514. Sara Baartman didn't have a number. Just her bones in a glass case with a note inside saying "Griqua".'

Jonah shook his head. 'Griqua is not the real name for my ancestors. They called themselves Khoikhoi – men of men. And her name isn't Sara Baartman.'

'How d'you know?'

'The people who stole her bones wouldn't have known her Khoi name.'

I nodded. 'They took her from Africa when she was young. They took her to England and then to France and made a show of her because she was different. When she died, they hung her skeleton in a museum. But I want to know where her spirit went.'

'The spirit goes home. Always home. Home to where it belongs.'

'So Sara Baartman's spirit is home now?'

He clicked his tongue. 'Don't call her that!'

I shot a glance at Jonah.

'Give her a real name. A Khoi name. So she knows she belongs. That she's back with her own people.'

'What name, then?'

Jonah was silent as he looked at the paintings above us. He seemed to be searching through the shapes looking for something. 'Star Song. So we'll hear her song.'

'But how will her spirit find its way home after all this time?'

He gave me a strange look. 'Perhaps that's why you have to go back.'

'Go back where?'

'To the woman.'

'Which woman?'

'The one with the children. The one on the plain.'

'What's she got to do with Sara Baartman?'

'She has to get home to the Red Desert.'

'What about the moon? It was supposed to carry her.'

'It's no longer a sickle. It's set her down.'

'Then the hunters will have to take her.'

'They can't. You heard them. They have to stay on the land that belonged to their father's father.'

'I don't believe all that!'

'It's true. They're frightened to move. In case someone claims their land. It's been stolen from them for hundreds of years. Even though they're the First People.'

'Stolen by whom?'

'By farmers. By other tribes. By mining people who've found diamonds on their land and want to get rich. Wherever they turn it gets taken from them. Eventually there'll be no place left for them.'

My head was spinning. 'What're we supposed to do?'

'You have to help her reach her people.'

'Me?'

'I can't come with you.'

'Why not?'

'The desert's too hot for cheetahs. There's not enough water.'

'Then it's too hot for me!'

'A gemsbok can survive in the desert. Your name is Spirit of the Desert. That's why you have to go.'

'I can't do it. I can't go alone.'

'I'll come part of the way with you.'

'And then?'

'The swallow will be with you.'

I shot a look at Jonah. 'The swallow? You mean Boskind?'

He nodded.

So it *was* them. It *was* Rebecca who had killed the hyena. Rebecca, the martial eagle! Rebecca, the Valkyrie!

Rebecca who could *be* anything! *Kill* anything! 'A swallow's just a tiny bird. It won't help. I need Rebecca.'

'She can't go.'

'Why not?'

'She's proved herself. She killed the hyena.'

'And I've proved myself too. I dived into the Hole.' I felt for the cowrie shell in my pocket. Cool and smooth under my fingers.

'It's not the same.'

I eyed him. 'Who makes these rules?'

Jonah shrugged. 'They're things I know.'

I stared back at his cheetah face. The high cheetah cheekbones. The fierce cheetah eyes. The strong cheetah chest. I thought of the jaws that could tear a windpipe. The sharp teeth that could rip the flesh off an antelope thigh. Snatch a heart from its cavity. I thought of the bloodied whiskers and panting mouth. The padded paws with their tearing claws.

I felt my fists clench. 'Is that what you are?'

'What?'

'A cheetah! Cruel and bloody!'

'Animals aren't cruel.'

'They kill!'

'Only when they have to. They're not like humans. Fish, you have to do this.'

163

My head whirled. My throat suddenly went dry. Already I was thirsty and I wasn't even in the Red Desert. I glanced around the cave. I looked at the paintings. They weren't moving. There was still time for another plan.

'Can't my father come with me? He knows the desert. He knows these people.'

'If your father went, how would it help you?'

'He'd know where to find water.'

'It's not your father who has to be tested. It's you, Fish! *You* need the power of their *!gi*' There was a change in Jonah's face. His eyes seemed urgent. He held both my hands. Squeezed them. 'You're Spirit of the Desert now. We all have an animal spirit. It's part of us. Like our soul. But we don't all find this spirit. You've been lucky. You've found yours. Only special people find theirs. Someone who has extra powers. Maybe one day you'll be a shaman.'

I shook my head. 'I don't want to be shaman!'

'A shaman is a special person. Someone who is full of *!gi*. A healer. Someone put on earth to make it a better place. To take the evil away.'

'I can't do that.'

'You can when you've been healed.'

'I'm not sick.'

'No, but . . .'

I stared back at him. 'But what, Jonah? What? What? What? What are you trying to say?'

'You're not sick. You're hurting and muddled. This journey will give you power. I promise!'

He let go of my hands. Picked up the musical bow. Put it to his chin and started to tap the string.

The music began wrapping its net around me. The animals and people on the walls were beginning to dance . . . or was it swim? The paintings were floating upwards. I heard their voices. Voices from the throats of hundreds and thousands of people coming to me. Echoing through the darkness of the cave.

If I could understand them, *if* I could only recognise something, *if* I could understand their song – they might help me on this journey.

The rock was becoming soft and transparent. I could feel my body changing.

22

Spirit of the Desert

We are moving through a strange terrain. Different to any I've seen before. Dark rocks with flattened tops show against a shimmering night-blue sky. We're running so fast, the stars seem to reel and rush across the huge vault above us. Jonah is sprinting alongside me without effort. Huge strides that make me stretch my legs to keep up with him.

'How will we find her?' My breath comes in gasps.

'We're following her tracks.'

'I don't see any.'

'Follow the signs.'

'What are you talking about? What signs?'

'When the animal stops, you must stop. When the animal jumps, you must jump. A hunter puts on the mind of the antelope or leopard he's hunting. Behaves like he behaves. Run like he runs. A hunter must *be* the animal.'

I glance at him. What secrets does he carry in his head? 'But we're not following an animal. It's a woman with three children we're looking for.'

He turns sharply to me. 'It's the same. Footprints or tracks make a pattern. The pattern makes a story in your head. Wind blurs a track. An insect crosses a footprint. Wind and insects are our timekeepers. They tell us how old the tracks are. How long since the animal or person passed. Tracking is a map you hold in your head. You know it like the footsteps of a dance. You know where to put your next foot without thinking.'

Jonah knows. He's setting the pace. Faster than I've ever run. But I'm not sure where my feet are going. My legs blur beneath me. We're running across a vast plain. Here and there I see the dark outline of another creature. Some scattered bones. A carcass. But there's no time to stop or investigate.

'Jonah, slow down! I can't keep up,' I pant next to him.

'You have to hurry. She needs water.'

'How'll I find water?'

'Follow the signs. You'll know them.'

'Rubbish!' I want to stamp my feet. '*How* will I know? I don't believe even *you* know.' The words come hot from the back of my throat. 'You've no idea where water is. You've tricked me into coming because *you* don't want to do it! So you say *I* must. And where's Boskind? You said he'd help me.'

'He'll come.'

'This far?'

'Distance is nothing for a swallow.'

The sky darkens to ink black. The stars make a broad milky path across it. Jonah stops to catch his breath. 'See that tight cluster there – they're important stars for you to recognise.'

I glare at him through slit eyes without answering. Still angry.

'You have to remember them.'

'Why?' I snarl.

'They're the Rain Stars. Or Thorn Stars. They prick the sky with their sharp barbs to bring the rain. Their husband is the Giant over there. See his belt.'

Jonah points to a pattern of bright stars. But I don't see any Giant. I don't even see his belt. I don't want to know any of this.

'The Giant was ordered to shoot the three Zebras over there. But he failed. So he was frozen into the sky with the Lion watching him. Now he can never pick up his bow to shoot the Lion. See, those two bright stars are the Lion's eyes staring at the Giant. But it's the Rain Stars you must remember. They're the important ones.'

'I don't care! I don't want to know!'

'And look out for *tsamma* melons that grow wild on the dunes. They're filled with juicy flesh.'

I snort hot air out through my nostrils. 'How am I supposed to recognize them?'

'Nothing else will be growing there.'

'Why're you telling me all this?'

'So you'll know what to do. And remember if you take something, give something in return. And watch out for the eland bull.'

I toss my head. 'An eland? I'm not afraid of an eland! My horns are longer. An eland wouldn't dare do battle with me!'

'You don't understand. The eland is the Rain Bull. The Sacred Antelope.'

'If he's the Rain Bull, he'll bring rain. That's good.'

'I'm warning you. Don't make him angry. His storms are fierce. They're not just rain storms! His voice is the thundering of the sky and the bellowing of the wind.'

A moon rises. Not a sickle. But full, round and huge. It floats up like a giant mother-of-pearl button. A web of light falls across my shoulders like a blanket. Ahead of us, the dunes heave in a silvery sea of sand. Wave upon wave of them. Far into the distance of the night. An endless sea of stormy sand.

Jonah stops. And suddenly I know he's stopped not to look at them, but because this is where his journey is ending. This is where he's going to leave me. And my heart stands still.

He bends his neck. Removes the creamy ostrich-shell necklace my father has given him. Then turns and places it over my head.

This is ridiculous. Animals don't wear necklaces! Yet I feel the warmth of his body in the tiny shell discs against my chest.

'The necklace will protect you.'

My anger vanishes. Suddenly I feel weak. I look at the sea of sand. I glance down at my feet. They seem too small for such a vast expanse. How will I manage? And when the sun rises where will I hide in the blistering heat?

I shake my head. It feels too heavy for my body. 'I need more than a necklace. I can't do this.'

'You must!'

'I don't want to. I'm frightened. I can't do it.'

'You must! You are Spirit of the Desert! You hold the stars between your horns!' His voice is fierce.

Then he turns and is gone. Far, far away in a streak of silvery shadow. I watch until he's just a speck that finally dissolves into nothing.

The sand ridges stretch in all directions in the bright moonlight. Featureless. Colourless. Lifeless and bleak beyond all imagination. I think of Rockwood. Of the house with its shell tower and the limpets and peri-winkles, all neatly patterned and laid out. And the little pieces of mirror reflecting the light of the stars. All waiting for me to come home. I think of sitting safely in the tower. Of the sea and the whales calling me. And I think of my father.

The stars stretch across the sky like a huge pale tent. But now they seem very far away. I'm alone and I have to find a woman and lead her to water. Soon the dawn will come and with it the heat.

I sense something irreversible has happened. A shudder runs through me. There is a presence of some-thing out there. Something shapeless and frightening that I still have to face.

Now the sky at the edge of the earth is touched by light. The sand turns from silver to cream. Suddenly,

171

like an arrow shot from the bow of the earth, the sun bursts above the horizon and the desert explodes in a sea of orange. So orange, whichever way I turn, my eyes are blasted by the colour.

The Red Desert. In all directions, nothing except sand and sun-bleached bones.

A wind curls gusts of sand off the ridge of a dune in front of me. Already the air against my face is hot and dry, scouring my eyes and nostrils. I turn to face into the wind. And as I turn, far in the distance I see a few dark specks moving against the sand.

23

The Rain Bull

Along the ridge of a red dune, the shapes waver. Sometimes real. Sometimes disappearing in the shimmer. Dancing through the heat like the figures in the cave paintings. I squint into the glare as they come closer. Then the woman emerges from the shimmering light and comes into the space ahead of me. Two skinny children follow. They walk towards me. Their feet are wrapped in the tattered remains of the *kaross*. Ripped and bound around their soles as a buffer to the blistering hot sand. The blanket with ostrich feathers is torn and fluttering in strips around their shoulders.

I know she has seen me even though I haven't moved. She searches my face. Then I see the silent baby strapped against her chest. Silent and absolutely still.

Where are the roots she is supposed to dig for?

Where are the secret sip-holes of water buried in the sand? And the green *tsamma* melons filled with soft juicy flesh? Where are they? How long can anyone survive without water?

My tongue is thick and swollen inside my mouth. I remember her words: *Hunger is not soft. We do not hunger gently.*

At the edge of the earth, huge puffy clouds gather heat. Even if the Rain Stars come out, no amount of pricking will bring rain from this white-hot sky. Black bird-shapes circle silently above. Around and around. Not martial eagles. But vultures. Now I understand. The woman clings to her lifeless baby because she can't give it up to the vultures.

Then I see a tiny bird darting below. A swallow?

The vultures circle lower. They come in clumsily and settle in a flurry of black feathers and scrawny pink necks, pecking and squawking at each other and rising up again as they fight to get closer. The swallow dives down, hurling its tiny body at them, aiming at their heads. But what use is a swallow against the long talons and ripping beaks? Nothing bothers them. More and more vultures make noisy landings.

I run at them. Toss my head. Snort hot air. Kick up sand. I try not to think of all of them settling on me at once, knocking me to the ground, pecking and gouging and eating me alive like ants swarming over an upturned beetle.

I stampede them. They take to the air lazily and settle again at a distance.

At the same moment, the swallow flies straight at the woman. It snatches a piece of ostrich feather from the shredded blanket, then swoops in again, to snatch another strand. Then it flies off and hovers over a shape in the sand. I squint into the light and see it's an animal skull. Nestled inside the smooth white bone is a nest made of the torn feathers. Lying against the feathers are three tiny eggs.

Three wondrous eggs. Speckled and glistening.

The woman scoops them up and holds them in the palm of her hand like fragile jewels. She searches the sky for the swallow. But it's gone. She carries the eggs to the children. With tiny careful movements, she cracks the shells. Squeezes the liquid yolk into their mouths. Gathers the dribbles that run down their chins and smooths it back between their lips. Then she sucks the broken shells.

I remember Jonah's words. *If you take something, give something in return.* I look around. The woman has nothing to give. The digging stick is broken. The *kaross* and ostrich-feather blanket are in shreds and the precious ostrich shells have to be kept in case she finds water.

All I have is Jonah's necklace. Then I remember the shell. The small, smooth cowrie shell in my pocket. Except now, it's under my tongue. I drop it on the sand next to the woman. It's strange to see a shell so far from the sea. For a moment our eyes meet. She seems to urge me.

The vultures are circling. I can drive them off again. But for how long?

I have to find water for her. I have to find the Rain Bull. But how? Again I think of what Jonah said.

You have to track an animal. A hunter becomes the animal. You put on the mind of the antelope or the leopard you're hunting. Behave like he behaves. Run like he runs. Jump like he jumps. The tracks make a pattern. The pattern makes a story in your head. Tracking is like dancing. You know where to put your next foot without even thinking.

I'm *not* sure . . . but I have to find the Rain Bull. Chase it down and challenge it to bring rain. My feet carry me towards the horizon where the clouds tower. I run and run. Up across the ridges and down into the hollows. The sun beats like an iron gong against my forehead. Into a place of hell with dry bones and scorching winds that draw swirling sandstorms into the sky.

Hopeless. It's utterly hopeless. I get no closer. The thick clouds billowing upwards along the horizon come no nearer. They race along the earth's edge with me.

I dash in circles. Stamping my feet. Kicking up the dust. Snorting. Hearing the sound of Jonah's *gorah*. Not soft and gentle now. But wild with twanging. I buck and swerve and charge. I bellow to the sound of the *gorah*. I demand the Rain Bull to show itself.

A storm of dust covers the sun. Curdles the clouds. The day turns dark. The sand of the Red Desert turns the colour of beaten brass. A green glow fills the air. Sharp arrows of lightning pierce the clouds. Zigzag down through the darkness and flash around me. They touch the earth with almighty cracks until the air crackles and fizzes with light and sound.

Suddenly I hear hooves drumming. A gigantic shape looms up out of the darkness. The shape thunders towards me through clouds of dust, snorting and bellowing and lowering its head as if to scoop me up and toss me out of its way like a twig.

The Rain Bull! The bull from the painting in the

cave. The same ochre colour with pale neck. A thick neck with swags of heavy flesh. The bull whose voice is the thundering of the sky and the bellowing of the wind.

I stamp my foot and thrust my head back. I am Spirit of the Desert. I hold the stars between my horns. So I stand my ground. Wait for it to pound into me.

At the last moment, the Rain Bull swerves and thunders past and I feel its burning breath sweep over me. Then it turns and comes back. Slowly, this time. Step by step. It squares its shoulders. Draws up all it strength into its thick, solid neck as it circles me. One leg scissoring sideways over the other with its head lowered as it keeps me in its sight.

I pivot with it and put out my tongue to taste the air between us. Then I lower my head and tense my body and wait for it to hurl itself at me. Wait for its lightning arrows to shrivel me up and burn me to nothing but ash.

When that moment comes, I thrust my head forward with all the strength my neck can bear. I feel the weight of my horns lift and arch upwards. They rip upwards in a sharp swoop. Tear at the air and pierce the sky.

There is a roar louder than the raging sea. Louder than all the sounds in my head. Blood pours down. Blinds me. Stops me in my tracks.

I shake the blood from my face. Taste it running down my cheeks. But it's not blood. It's rain. Warm like blood. It thuds against the sand and blots out the bellows of the Rain Bull. I stamp my feet and dance to the rhythm of the drumbeats against the earth.

The rain beats down and drenches me. Suddenly my body feels heavy and my legs tired. The weight of my head and horns and rain-sodden skin are too much. I'm so tired I can hardly stand. I close my eyes while the storm batters me and I lean into the wind and rain.

It's hard to say how long the storm lasts. In the quietness afterwards, the earth is cool and the air smells sweet with moisture. When I open my eyes, there is light everywhere. A strange soft glow shimmers along lines that stretch far into the desert. A string of light draws me forward. I look over my shoulder. Behind me another line of light stretches backwards to the woman and her children.

In single file, we follow the lines. They make a pathway across the sand for us to tread on. With each footstep we know exactly where the next must go. My feet are dancing forward now. We're hunters following a track. This is the path that takes us where we need to be.

It takes us to the top of the highest dune. In the hollow below is a group of people. Men and women sitting around a fire and children playing in the sand. They see us coming and jump up to meet us. They gather around the woman and lift the two children high into the air, speaking in excited clicks. We are drawn into their circle. They clap and dance and sing. The seed rattles around their ankles make a *shirr-shirr* music and their *gorah* twangs out over the dunes. The clapping and chanting sounds like the heartbeat of the desert.

Their daughter has come home.

She tells the story of a husband too young to grow a beard, who didn't see his friend's arrow coming at him through the ostrich's dust.

An old man touches the women's shoulder. He's seen that she is sick. As he holds her, his body starts to shake. He sings out into the night. He is taking her pain into himself. It shivers through him. He draws her suffering from her. Finally the last words have been sung and he falls down, exhausted.

The fire burns down to a pile of smoking ash and weary flame. A silence spreads through the group.

In the cool breeze at my back I sense the sea far, far away. I turn to leave.

Then my eye catches a movement. A single streak of light sweeping the sky. A falling star. Brighter here in the desert than ever before. A rush of sound fills the air. A sound so loud the sky seems to be vibrating – humming as if the gigantic bow of the earth has been twanged.

Around the circle everyone listens.

Across the embers the woman is looking at me. And in her look I know she is not just the wife of the ostrich-hunter who has found her clan. She's also the spirit of another woman. She is Star Song.

Her journey is over. Her spirit is home.

ST. ALOYSIUS COLLEGE LIBRARY

24

Vanessa

I stood at the edge of the sea with the piece of wood tracing Vanessa's name with the point of it in the wet sand.

This time I wrote her name in huge cursive letters so the 'V' and 'a' and 'n' and '$essa$' all flowed easily together. Cursive writing is better for Vanessa's name. There are no sharp points. No snake 'S's. Only full round curves and the double 'ss' making a link-pattern that could go on and on for ever.

Strange . . . all the time in the Red Desert I hadn't thought of Vanessa. I'd known what to do. I hadn't needed any of her words to tell me. I'd found the Rain Bull myself. Discovered the lines of light and found the clan. And seen the spirit of Star Song returned to where she belonged.

I'd done all these things on my own.

Now I could hear the whales calling. This time not *Ffishhh . . . Ffishhh . . . Ffishhh . . !* But *Vanesssa . . !*

I lifted my arm to fling the piece of wood into the sea. Ready to toss it into the water. It belonged there. Maybe it would go with the whales. Float all the way back to the icy Antarctic with the whales.

'Vanessa . . .?'

Suddenly, I realised it truly was someone calling.

I turned. My father was coming across the beach.

'Vanessa? You've been gone a long time. I've looked everywhere for you. Where've you been?'

I searched his face. Would he understand if I told him the truth? If I told him where I'd really been? The Red Desert and the Rain Bull and the woman looking at me across the fire were too strange to explain. Where would my story begin?

'Vanessa?'

'Why're you calling me Vanessa?'

'That's who you are.'

'You know I prefer to be called Fish.'

'Who are you today then? Fish or Vanessa?'

I looked back at him sharply. 'What do you mean?'

'Fish . . . I know.'

'Know what?'

'I know where that piece of wood comes from.'

183

'You followed me?'

'No. I saw you one day when I was in the graveyard.'

'Saw me?'

He nodded. 'Beneath the milkwood tree.'

I searched his face, looking for clues. How much did he know?

'I understand.'

'Understand what?'

'I know why you made a special place under the milkwood tree.'

I looked down. Scratched a wide circle around the letters in the sand. I waited for him to say something. But he didn't. When he had been silent for too long, I stole a look at him. 'So . . . why? Why did I do it?'

'Because you weren't ready.'

'Ready for what?'

'To leave Mum.'

Silence. Not even a whale calling now. I glanced at him from the corner of my eye, watching to see if he really understood. When I knew he wasn't going to say anything more, I spoke. 'I didn't want her to be all alone. The graveyard seemed a lonely place. I put Vanessa there to keep her company.'

He turned and put his hand on my shoulder. Looked straight at me. 'Yes . . . I know . . . except it wasn't really Vanessa, was it? She wasn't really there. It was just a piece of wood. The real Vanessa is here in front of me.'

I picked at a splinter in the wood with my nail. Not wanting to look at him. The splinter tore my finger. I watched a bead of blood appear. 'Yes. But now I know.'

'Know what?'

'Mum's not there in the graveyard, is she? Her body's there but her spirit's not.'

'Where is she, then?'

I sensed my father watching me. Willing me to look up at him. But I couldn't. I sucked my finger to stop it bleeding. The tinny taste of blood caught the back of my throat and made my eyes water.

'Fish?'

'She's here. On this beach. Right now. Wherever we are. Her spirit is with us. She doesn't need the other Vanessa.' My voice seemed croaky and rough. 'That other, imaginary Vanessa – she doesn't need her, does she?'

He shook his head. 'No.'

I blinked hard and looked back at him then. 'That's what I thought. That's why I took the wood away.'

'What're you going to do with it?'

'Throw it into the sea where it belongs.'

'Why? It's just a bit of wood from an apple box.'

'I know. But . . .' I scratched through the writing on the sand. A wave would soon come and smooth it all away.

'But what?'

'I should've stayed in the sea. If I couldn't save Mum, perhaps I should've drowned with her.'

'What?'

'I'm a strong swimmer. I should've saved her.'

'Is that what you believe, Fish? That because you didn't save Mum, you need to be back in the sea? Is that what you believe?' He drew me into his arms.

I shook my head. 'Not any more. That was before.'

'Before what?

'Before I . . .' The words dried up in my mouth. There was so much to tell him. About the Cave and the paintings and the journey and the Red Desert and the Rain Bull and the woman. It was much too much to tell in a short moment. And perhaps . . .? I glanced up at his face. Perhaps he knew already.

'Before what?'

'Before I heard the star's song.'

My father nodded. Then I saw the smile at the corners of his mouth as he looked at me. 'Do you think we should take the boat out again sometime? Before it rots completely? We could throw out some lines. Perhaps while we wait for the fish to bite, you can tell me where you've been all this while.'

25

The Joining

I don't go up into the stone tower much any more. I don't seem to need the stone walls with their layers of shells or the bits of mirrors that reflect back the stars. I don't want to sit in the small space of the tower – to be a snail in a snail house – and see the stars reflect back in the mirrors.

I want to lie out on the beach on my back with my arms spread wide and feel the inky-dark sky stretching in all directions. Huge. Bigger than anyone can imagine. With a myriad of stars. All around me. Until I'm dizzy.

How can the sky go on and on for ever? How can there be so many stars?

I can feel the earth spinning around me. Weaving a magic stronger than dust. Stronger than words. Jonah was right. The stars do sing. They sing not just one story but many stories. And their songs have taken thousand of years to reach us. I'm hearing songs from long ago when the earth was just beginning.

And even though I can't understand it all – even though it seems strange – I've written it down in the book called *Fish Notes* and I've added the words *and Star Songs* to the cover. I've told of the mysterious things the four of us experienced when we passed through the wall of the cave and went into another world.

Afterwards, all four of us went back to the cave. We crawled under the rock shelf and collected in the part of the cave where Heart Fire lay half buried below the paintings. All four of us – Jonah, Rebecca, Sweet and I. Except Sweet was not yet Sweet, nor was he Sebastian, whose name was whispered by the trees. He was still the small boy with the name Boskind.

We had brought home the spirits of all who needed to be brought home. More than that, we had brought home our own spirits. And because of this, I kept the piece of wood with 'Vanessa' written on it to remind me that at different times even though we think we are different people, we're really the same. Just fighting with ourselves to understand ourselves.

The four of us went back to the cave and sat there

with Heart Fire, not touching anything of his, except to each add another stone to his pile of sacred stones. This was our farewell to him. And although Jonah had already placed a stone there long before, he took another egg-shaped one from the gully. Sweet, who was not yet Sweet, found a forest stone covered with curling bits of green-grey lichen. And Rebecca put down one of Og's eggs – not really a stone, but stone-shaped and precious.

I thought of bringing a stone from the tower, but in the end I put down a stone that was more meaningful. A piece of my father's pink rose quartz from the Red Desert. A reminder of where Heart Fire's wife and children had found her people.

And I brought the paintings. I took them down from the walls of Rockwood. Each one of them. The paintings of ships and fish souls and storms. All the paintings I've ever painted. I spread them around Heart Fire so he was surrounded by rock paintings and sea paintings.

Then Jonah began to play his *gorah*. And as the music filled the cave and echoed around our heads we heard a hum. It was the boy – the small boy singing. At first it was just sounds. Croaky sounds that seemed to come out of a dry throat needing water. But the sounds turned to words and the words to stories.

He sang of his sister Rebecca, the martial eagle, who had killed the hyena. He sang of the journey to the desert. Of the three eggs he'd found. He sang of the creatures of the forest. And of the trees themselves and the sounds they whispered . . . *Sebastian* . . . *Sebastian* . . . *Sebastian* . . . Last of all, he sang of his father.

And when his song was finished, we realised Jonah had long stopped playing. The music in the cave was just the sweet sound of the boy's voice telling stories he'd stored up for too long.

'Sweet,' Rebecca smiled and hugged him to her. 'Your name is Sweet.'

'Sweet . . .' said the boy as he rolled the sound around his mouth testing his new name shyly.

'Yes, Sweet,' I whispered.

Jonah nodded.

Whether it was the candlelight, or the sound of Sweet's song, I'm not sure, but the people in the rock paintings with their strange animal heads began to move along the lines of yellow light.

Then something more mysterious happened. The ships in my paintings began to move. They jibbed and sailed and floated. They joined the rock painting of the ship with the flag that flew in the wrong direction. Everything became watery. The ships sailed between the people. And the people danced between the ships. It didn't seem to matter which belonged to what. What was sea world, earth world, or sky world.

And voices from the throats of thousands and thousands of souls filled the cavity of rock, all coming together with Sweet's story.

It was all one.

A joining.

'Marvellous! Bloody marvellous!' whispered Rebecca.

And I knew then what I know now, as I lie here on the beach under the stars . . . that you can never kill the spirit. The spirit is truly something marvellous.

It's always alive no matter how long you've been dead.

Whether Sara Baartman is Sara, or Star Song, or whatever she's called, she isn't the box of bones and the bottles of brain and insides that came back to Africa. She's the spirit that has always been alive.

She's the voice in the stones and the sand and the sea and the sky and the stars.

Nothing can destroy her. Nothing.

Not the people who captured her and took her away. Nor the people who displayed her bones in the museum after she died.

Nothing can kill the spirit.

So that day in the cave we left behind not just stones and paintings, but something more. On that day, we stood high on the dunes and looked back. We watched the waves crashing in a solid line of foam along the curve of white sand. Then we turned and faced south. We gave our last look towards the cave and the white water licking the rocks below.

We saluted the cave and all that was hidden inside it. All that would stay hidden.

We'd rolled heavy stones across the narrow ledge opening into the other secret cave. We'd packed the stones hard against each other and pushed sand up against them so there'd be no sign of another deeper cave where Heart Fire lay.

We left him in his sacred space with his fragile bones and fragile skin *kaross* where no one would disturb him – surrounded by the paintings of his people going on a spiritual journey. Left him dreaming of his wife and his children.

Afterwards, we stood on the dunes for a long time, each with our own thoughts and the memory of what had happened there. And while we watched, the sun caught the cliff face of the Gap and sent back a pink glow. And I knew the rocks and the cave with its mysteries were still alive.

There was no looking back. We sang the songs we carried in our hearts. They were part of us now.

Then we turned. Rebecca led up front. An ostrich feather stuck out from her wild ginger hair as it made a halo against the sun. Then Jonah, Sweet and I followed behind.

Now Jonah has come to stay at Rockwood. There is nothing that holds him to the cave. He knows his ancestors' spirits are part of him, wherever he goes. And Sweet has come as well. He has shown us the secret silk nests of the hunting spider and where the rinkhals hides under the wooden deck of Rockwood and how quietly the puff-adder lies in the sun next to the path up the cliff.

They have both come to stay, Jonah and Sweet. But not Rebecca. What would a green-eyed wildcat do, trapped in a house like Rockwood? No, Rebecca still lives out in the wide-open space of the dunes.

But the boat *Swiftsure* has been painted. The sails are mended. And on quiet evenings my father and the four of us take her out into the Bay and throw a line out and fish. And one of these days when the winds are right we'll sail out past Whale Point and see who'll be the first to spot the whales returning.

*

All this I've written in this book with the words *Fish Notes and Star Songs* on the front cover. And I've made a list of some of the names in the story. The list is not because I want to pin things down like a butterfly or a strange insect on a display board, but because I want to understand more. If you know the true meaning of something then you begin to understand that a name is not just a label but much more.

An *arikreukel* (ari crickle) is a large sea snail which you can eat. It has a crinkled disc or lid that it pulls tight when it goes inside its shell. Its Latin name is *Turbo sarmaticus*.

A *bluebottle* is a small floating sea creature with stinging tentacles. It has a clear blue bubble that helps it drift on the surface of the sea. It's also called a Portuguese man-of-war because it looks like a small ship sailing under full sail. Its Latin name is *Physalia Physali*.

The *boubou* is a secretive bird that calls a duet with its mate: *Boo-boo* followed by *whee-oo*.
Buchu (boo gu) is a plant with small leaves that have a

strong smell when you crush them. It's used to make herbal medicine and tea.

A *dassie* (das see) is a creature like a rock rabbit. It eats grass and lives in groups in caves and rocky places. The name comes from the Dutch word *das* which means a badger, but a dassie is not a real badger.

Fynbos (fain bos) is a mixture of plants with small leaves that grow wild next to the coast and on the mountains of South Africa. It is one of the six special plant kingdoms in the world. The word comes from Dutch and means fine bush.

A *gemsbok* (it has a soft 'g' like in French) is an antelope found in the dry desert regions of South Africa. It has very strong black and white face markings and long sword-like black horns. It comes from a mixture of the French word *chamois* which is also a type of antelope and the Dutch word *bok* which means buck. Its Latin name is *Oryx gazella*.

The *gorah* (gore ra) is an African musical instrument shaped like a bow with string tied between the two ends. The string vibrates when you strike it with a stick. Sometimes the bow is rested against a hollow gourd to make the sound louder.

The *Griqua* (gri kwa) were one of the original hunter groups living in southern Africa. The *kwa* sound comes from the name they call themselves – *Khoi,* or *Khoikhoi,* (coy coy) which means 'Men of men'. They speak with a click language. The Bushmen or *San* people share a similar language. In click languages the ! and / and ' in words stand for certain click sounds. Together the group is called *Khoisan* (coy san). *San* means 'Men without land'. But the Bushmen prefer to be called by their real clan names like !Kung and Ju/'hoan, which tells who they are and where they come from. Some people think of them as still wearing skins and hunting but they don't. They live a very hard life trying to earn a living in the driest parts of southern Africa. They are still 'people without land'.

A *kaross* is a cover or blanket made of softened animal skin. The word sounds soft like the feel of an animal.

A *meerkat* is an African mongoose that eats lizards and mice. Its name comes from the Dutch words *meer,* which means sea, and *kat,* which means cat. But a meercat is not a sea creature. It lives in small burrows in the ground. Its Latin name is *Suricata suricatta*.

A *puff-adder* is a large, thick, poisonous snake with a triangular head. It's lazy during the day and hunts at night. It puffs itself up when it's about to attack.

A *rinkhals* (wrink als) is a spitting cobra which raises its body and spreads its hood when it attacks. It has a cream ring around its neck. The name comes from the Dutch words *rink* which means ring and *hals* which means neck.

A *tsamma* is a fleshy melon that grows on creeping vines in the desert. You have to say it with your tongue clicking against the front of your palate on the 't'.

A *vlei* (flay) is a marshy area usually in a valley. It comes from the Dutch word *vallei* which means valley.

And who is *Sara Baartman*? She was a real person born in 1789 in South Africa who worked as a servant. She was persuaded by an English doctor to return with him to England where he made money for himself by displaying her to curious people. She was paraded at circuses and museums and parties, often in a cage, and she was later put on show in Paris. She became a non-person, robbed not only of her real Khoi name, but also of her identity as a human being.

When she died in 1816, aged 27, she was 'owned' by an animal trainer. After her death, a plaster cast was made of her body, then her organs were removed for display and her skeleton was hung in a museum in Paris. It stayed there until 2002 when the French Government passed a law which allowed her remains to be returned to her homeland and her people. Her right to be treated with dignity was finally given back to her after 200 years.

ST. ALOYSIUS COLLEGE LIBRARY